SURGEO

KATE ASHTON

MILLS & BOON LIMITED
London · Sydney · Toronto

First published in Great Britain 1983
by Mills & Boon Limited, 15–16 Brook's Mews,
London W1A 1DR

Australian copyright 1983
Philippine copyright 1983

ISBN 0 263 74442 6

Set in 10 on 11 pt Linotron Times
03/1083–59,850

Photoset by Rowland Phototypesetting Ltd
Bury St Edmunds, Suffolk
Made and printed in Great Britain by
Richard Clay (The Chaucer Press) Ltd
Bungay, Suffolk

CHAPTER ONE

THE autumn suited Claire. She breathed in a deep draught of air, heavy with the scent of the wet earth, and left the path to trudge through the first carpet of burnished leaves on the floor of the park.

Their colours reflected the copper and bronze lights in Claire's hair; the brown of the resting trees matched her eyes and the quietness of autumn's relinquished energy fitted perfectly with her sense of peace and rest after a hectic nine days on the kidney unit. It was a day off and she luxuriated in the thought of the hours stretching ahead of her. Her flatmate was in the middle of a long run of duty, with emergency cover of her own and the twin theatre, and Claire unashamedly anticipated with pleasure the peace and quiet of the flat. Fiona was a darling, but sometimes Claire felt as if she was living at the centre of a tornado with her friend.

Claire paused and watched while a small grey squirrel foraged busily at the base of a tree, then, becoming aware of her, looked round bright-eyed before streaking up into the branches and out of sight. Yes, she thought, I quite agree with you, that's how people often make me feel too. She smiled at the comparison between herself and the little creature. It was apt. Claire was as reserved, self-contained and shy as her flatmate was open, brash and outgoing and, mostly, this unlikely combination made for a very happy partnership.

Claire kicked a ball back to the group of children who were playing football on soggy ground beside the path, then left the park through huge black wrought iron gates and made for the shopping centre.

Elchester was a small town, proud of the new pedestrian centre which boasted branches of all the main chain stores as well as a host of smaller shops re-housed from their positions along the winding old high street.

With plenty of time to browse and make her choice, Claire wandered past the fountain with its naked cherubs and surrounding bare saplings, and into the main shopping arcade. She would look now and buy on her way back from the dentist.

The main reason for her outing was her check-up at the dentist, but the reason for the shopping trip was the marriage next week of the staff nurse on the unit. Claire had collected thirty pounds from the medical and nursing staff for a present for Sue, who was as popular among the staff as she was among the patients. Claire had managed to persuade her to stay on after she got married and to go on working full-time until she had to leave to have a family and Claire hoped that that would not happen too soon. She admired Sue's work and wanted her to consolidate her career.

Claire wondered often whether it was fair to feel like this on someone else's behalf. Perhaps, she thought, as she stared into the windows of a shop selling crystal and glass, I am turning into a career-orientated old maid, like Humph. She considered the nursing officer, Miss Humphreys, with a strange mixture of horror and affection. The crystal sparkled and shone in the autumn sunshine. A fruit bowl perhaps, mused Claire.

Marriage looked so effortless the way it had happened for Sue. She had met her fiancé while she was working on Casualty as a nineteen-year-old student nurse. He had been a policeman on night duty and they had met over the tragi-comic figure of a drunken road-traffic accident victim.

Now, two years later, they had their house, some modest furniture and a little old car and they were as happy as larks. Sometimes Claire felt that they inhabited a different planet from hers, a world in which men and women met and married with fairy-tale ease.

Fiona belonged to the same world. She did not avoid parties and sit at home reading instead, she did not think twice about spending all her salary on clothes and holidays in Spain, or accepting dates and two-timing them if it suited her. Yet, at twenty-six, Claire lived for her work as Sister on the kidney unit at St Helen's, as if for her, the outside world had stopped that dreadful day five years ago and then gone on turning without her.

Claire pushed these thoughts to the back of her mind. She had reached the Victorian house on the other side of the precinct where her dentist had his surgery and she pressed a brass bell on the polished panel outside the door and entered the familiar waiting-room from a tiled hall. She did not mind the dentist. She had been coming to Mr Payne ever since she was a little girl, and, belying his name, the old dentist was kind, reassuring and gentle.

In fact, she remembered with pleasure the visits to Elchester with her parents to go to the dentist because there had always been a treat associated with them— tea at the tea-room where you could have chocolate eclairs and drink tea out of flowered china. And because she had been taken regularly, she rarely, nowadays, had to have anything done after her half-yearly checks.

There were two people in the waiting-room, whose large bay windows, overlooking gardens at the back of the terrace, were like a picture in a gallery today, with the autumn leaves shining behind them. In front of the windows, on one of the row of wooden chairs facing her as she entered the room, sat a pale, thin girl, obviously in pain. She sat forward on her chair, a magazine open and unread on her lap, cradling her jaw in both hands and rocking back and forth in her chair. Claire, who had never had toothache, felt very sorry for her.

She took a magazine herself from the untidy pile on the table in the middle of the room and opened it automatically. She glanced around to her right, deciding where to sit, and registered with shock the man sitting in the middle of the row of chairs along that wall.

She hardly had time to look properly at the stranger before a blonde-haired girl in a white coat put her head around the door and gestured to him to follow her. The door shut quietly behind him.

Claire walked to the chair next to the one that he had just vacated and sat down heavily. It could not be him. Yet the walk had been the same; that rather earnest walk and the way he got up with his hands still in his pockets. The dark curly hair was the same. The strong face with its full mouth and straight nose, although pale—she could have sworn it was the same.

It must be a trick of fate, a strange reminder in this faintly clinical atmosphere that had brought his memory flooding back to her, Claire thought. Or the fact that she had been thinking about the past while she window-shopped on her way here. But, whatever it was that had stirred her, it could not be him. He had left Elchester five long years ago.

Claire's mind flew back to that first morning that she had gone on duty in the new bright blue uniform of staff nurse. She had walked on to the medical ward and had been met by the furious ward sister brandishing a drug chart.

Claire had walked quietly up to the desk and the sister had blazed at her, 'Look at this, Nurse, I mean Staff Nurse, just look at this! How often have I told that wretched houseman to get his lazy backside out of bed and sign drug charts? And now the night nurse has given this Omnopon without a covering signature and the blessed man's gone and left the ward without bothering his head to come and sign for it. They're not fit to be dustmen, never mind doctors, nowadays . . .'

'Yes, Sister,' was all Claire could think of to say to this diatribe. Sister was right, of course, the drug should never have been prescribed over the telephone, given and written up by the night nurse without a medical signature.

But that was hardly Claire's fault. She waited until the sister had calmed down. She knew that telling somebody was enough to effect a dramatic change in Sister Eliot, and sure enough, the volatile Irish sister's voice fell and the grey curls were patted as if there was a stray one that needed to be tucked under the pristine cap, which there was not.

'Well, let's hope the next one is an improvement,' the senior sister told her young colleague, nodding in a dignified way over her shoulder towards the doctors' room, 'although goodness knows, I haven't much hope. Your blue suits you, Nurse.' The last remark was almost submerged in the rest of her message, but there was just the suggestion of a smile around the sister's lips. Claire knew that this was the nearest to a congratulatory message that she'd received from this quarter.

'Will you tell that girl to come and give us the report?'

Claire had fetched the night nurse who was cowering in the sluice, avoiding Sister's wrath. She knew that she'd been put in an invidious position by the young houseman who had been determined not to leave his bed but to start fresh on his new ward this morning. But, although she knew that the ward sister knew this too, she had already been told off by night sister and she did not fancy any more undeserved rage coming her way after a long and exhausting night on duty.

It's probably the most gruelling experience of the whole training, Claire reflected, grinning at the sheepish night nurse, far too much responsibility and no real authority when it came to medical staff.

'And now can you get something done about this, Staff?' Sister had handed her the offending chart as soon as the report was over. It was a test, Claire knew, of her new authority as well as that of the new houseman.

She had gone into the doctors' room and found the big, unfamiliar figure of the new doctor bent over a trolley full of casenotes. He had turned as she came in and she had seen for the first time the deep grey eyes under fine brows, the calm expression, and felt the strong effect of his gaze. He had smiled, shyly, but steadily at her.

'How can I possibly learn all of these before the round?' he shrugged hopelessly at the laden trolley. 'I hate the first day.' She detected the softest trace of a Scottish lilt in his voice.

'I know, but it soon passes,' Claire had answered feelingly, the burden of her new responsibility lying heavily across her newly blue-uniformed shoulders.

Suddenly, when you became a staff nurse, the mistakes you made yesterday as a student were inexcusable, you became a fount of all knowledge for patients, relatives and students alike, and Sister handed you the ward keys with an air of confidence that made your knees weak.

She handed the young doctor the chart she held and he took it and looked at it, his eyes alighting at once upon the unsigned item at the end.

'Omnopon 10 mgs, im.p.r.n.,' he read, 'whose writing is this?'

'The night nurse's,' Claire admitted apologetically.

'Has he had any?'

'Yes, the night nurse gave him 10 mgs at five this morning after getting the order over the 'phone and the doctor promised to come and sign for it at once. He didn't turn up and I don't suppose he will now,' Claire told him.

'I'll come and look at the patient and check the DDA book and then write it up properly for you, Staff,' the new doctor promised her.

'Thank you,' she read 'Doctor Duncan' on a hastily written temporary badge on his lapel, 'Dr Duncan'. It must be his first ward, she thought.

He smiled at her rather nervously, as if he was reading her mind.

'I'm not quite used to my title yet,' he admitted.

'Oh, aren't you?' Claire blushed slightly and said, before she had time to think about her professional coolness, 'neither am I.'

She saw the question in his eyes.

'This is my first day as a staff nurse,' she said simply.

'Oh, congratulations,' he looked in turn at her badge, 'Staff Nurse Brown.'

He looked at her for a moment, taking in her soft shining hair, clear skin and deep brown eyes.

'I shall try not to mind getting out of bed at night,' he undertook, 'but I can't promise not to have other infuriating habits.' His smile turned into a grin. 'What is Sister like?'

'Cross,' said Claire, returning his smile, 'and pessimistic about the new breed of doctors.'

'I'd better watch my step in that case,' he again bent over the casenotes to find those belonging to the patient who had had the Omnopon, then followed Claire out into the ward.

'So that's him, is it?' Sister Eliot stated, the moment Claire reappeared at the desk. Sister stared furiously over at the bed where Dr Duncan now stood talking to a patient, and then made for the bedside with positive steps and a set face.

Claire was finishing the drug round when she was

summoned for a ward round and afterwards, as they drank coffee in her room, Sister Eliot grudgingly said, 'I suppose he might be all right.' This was praise indeed.

Dr Duncan had evidently passed his first test. The ward round had gone smoothly and Sister had been impressed by the prompt action he had taken to remedy his colleague's oversight with the drug, making no attempt to excuse his colleague but, at the same time, not pretending that it could not have been his fault.

And Claire had passed her first test too. After that the days melted into one another in her memory. There had been many when she had been in sole charge of the ward during Sister's days off and Dr Duncan had been medical cover for the ward. She remembered how he always seemed to have time to talk to relatives and patients, to teach the student nurses and to answer her queries and concerns. And he had never, ever refused to get up to see a patient in the night. He had been as good as his word—and better.

She remembered too the afternoon that they had spent resuscitating a little old diabetic lady who had fallen into a coma after consuming a number of chocolates from a secret hoard in her locker.

A student nurse had been tidying the patients' beds before the afternoon visitors when she had noticed how drowsy the old lady was and a strange nail-varnishy smell of acetone around her bed. She had alerted Claire to the state of the usually bouncy patient, and there had been a frantic effort to restore her blood sugar and insulin levels.

They had worked until long after Claire was due off duty and the evening staff were beginning the early evening routines in the ward. Dr Duncan had come and held her lightly by the shoulder as she was quietly leaving the ward.

'You looked as if you were perfectly determined that

we shouldn't lose her,' he said gently, and she had turned and looked frankly at him.

'Oh, I was,' she said.

'You're very involved in your work, aren't you, Staff,' he asked her thoughtfully.

'Yes . . . but . . . well, not too involved,' she answered defensively. And then she added before she realised that her remark would be revealing of her personal life, 'I'm fond of Mrs Smith. She reminds me of my mother.'

'Does she?' he returned.

'Anyway, there is nothing wrong with involvement in one's work,' Claire told him.

'Absolutely not,' he confirmed. 'One of our professors was enlightened enough to teach us that one cannot care without feeling and I always remember that. There is no time for real involvement in surgery and that's why I prefer medicine.'

'Me too,' Claire said.

'You look tired,' he told her, 'I'll walk with you to the Nurses' Home.'

'How do you know where I live?' she asked, surprised.

'I looked on the notice board in Sister's room,' he said, amused, 'where I was dispatched by that good lady to acquaint my dim medical self with the names and telephone numbers of senior nursing staff in case I should ever need to call them for an emergency in the ward. I knew the exercise would have more immediate benefits and I took note of your name and number especially.'

Claire felt the colour rising to her face again. She looked away to try to conceal the fact from him.

'Come on. I have to get home to my poor old mother. She'll be wondering where I am.'

'You live with your mother?' Claire could not hide the surprise in her voice.

He nodded and appeared to accept her surprise. It was an unfashionable way to live for a young man. She had supposed . . . what had she supposed? That he was perhaps married, or engaged, or living in a flat with a crowd of rowdy young doctors celebrating the end of their student days with endless parties and late-night adventures?

She didn't know. But she did know that she felt secretly pleased that this was the way he lived. Being herself the only child of parents who had had her late in life, having longed for their marriage to be blessed with a child for many years, Claire could identify with deep commitment to parents. She had taken it for granted that she would care for hers into their old age, just as she had been loved and cared for until she had left home to begin her nursing career. Even then she had spent all her days off and holidays with them, returning to the pretty cottage outside Elchester that they had lived in all their lives, and the room which she so loved and which still was very much her own.

Dr Duncan and she had, once or twice, found that their lunch breaks coincided. They had spent them together in a quiet corner of the hospital canteen, trying to ignore the looks and giggles of the student nurses on the ward who enjoyed speculation when they thought they were not being noticed. Although both were shy, Dr Duncan and Claire had established their relationship on first-name terms and looked forward very much to their snatched moments of semi-privacy.

And then three months after they had first met on the ward, he had found her arranging flowers in a sluice. She had shivered to find him behind her, a shiver of both nervousness and pleasant anticipation. She was arranging white carnations in an ugly cut glass vase. She indicated the shape of the hospital vase and said, as he came and stood behind her,

'Where do Supplies find them?'

'Pretty hideous, I must say,' he agreed, 'but compensated for by the tender touch of the flower arranger.'

Claire could not hide the flush this time. She also thought her knees were going to give way, but they didn't, they simply went numb. David Duncan was not the sort of man who handed out empty compliments.

'Claire, I've been going to ask you . . . I mean, I wondered if . . .' he stopped and so did Claire's heart.

He picked up a red carnation which lay among the loose bunch on the surface in front of them. He reached past her as if to pick it up and add it to the flowers already in the vase, but Claire snatched it out of his hand and burst out,

'Don't put that in there, David.' His hand dropped to his side and he looked at her, amazed and hurt. The mood of a moment ago vanished.

'Why, what's the matter Claire?' he asked.

'It's just that you must never, ever, put red flowers in with white ones,' she said miserably. Her hand was shaking, still holding the red carnation.

'Why on earth not?'

'It's just a very old superstition,' she stammered, agonised, wishing she had never begun to explain, 'something will happen to one of the patients, or to someone on the ward. You mustn't put those particular two colours together.'

David apologised in a low voice and handed her a white carnation, leaving her to put it where she would in the vase.

Sister Eliot chose that moment to call Claire to come and talk to Mr Smith, the husband of the diabetic lady, on the pretext that as she had been there when the old lady collapsed, she was the best person to tell him how much better she was now. Claire had a shrewd suspicion that Sister Eliot disapproved of the happy working

relationship that had developed between her and Dr
Duncan, not because it was not all she could wish
professionally, but because she feared where else it
might lead her favourite staff nurse. This wasn't the first
time she had called Claire away from a conversation with
the new houseman.

'The doctor can finish the flowers,' Sister said, mischievously, a smile softening her features.

Dr Duncan returned the smile with candid charm and
told her that he would make a poor job of them even if he
were to try. He had followed Claire to talk to Mr Smith
as Sister looked on, for once powerless to disapprove.

An hour or so later, Claire crossed the cobbled quadrangle between the medical block and the back entrance
of the Nurses' Home with a pleasant sense of satisfaction. Mr Smith had been delighted to find his wife
returned to her normal chirpy self, Sister was making life
generally pleasant for her on the ward and giving her lots
of responsibility, which she thrived on, and Dr Duncan
was there, more and more at the back of her mind while
she was off duty as well as at the front of it while she was
on. His quiet professional assurance and the gentle
relaxed companionship which they shared in odd moments of non-professional contact combined to make
him by far the nicest man she had ever met—or ever
wanted to meet. Claire felt that she was at a beautiful
crossroads in her life.

She turned into the long corridor that led to the main
entrance and off which, at either side, opened up a
staircase to the rooms on four floors. She had reached
the bottom of her flight of stairs when she saw the Home
Sister hurrying out of her room and approaching her
with a look of deepening concern.

'What on earth is it, Sister?' Claire asked, alarmed at
her expression.

'Staff Nurse Brown, my dear, I'm glad to have caught

you before you went to your room. I have just this minute received some bad news, for you, I'm afraid.'

She put her arm around Claire's shoulder and led her to her room at the end of the corridor. 'There is a telegram, about your parents. Try to keep calm.'

It had indeed arrived that minute. Claire could see the receding figure of the Post Office telegram man on his bicycle through the window of Home Sister's room.

She read and re-read the message in mute shock. There had been an accident involving the car her parents were travelling in on their holiday in Scotland. She was given the address and telephone number of the hospital and was advised to get there as soon as possible.

It was as quick to get the train as it was to try to reach an airport from Elchester and then get from the airport the other end to the hospital. Her heart stumbling in panic, she caught the next train and worried all the way. The nearer she got to her destination the stronger grew her sense of foreboding.

She was too late.

She had returned to the little cottage and had spent three numb weeks there on compassionate leave from St Helen's, doing all the terrible things that had to be done and, eventually, putting the cottage on the market, certain that she never wanted to spend another day or night there.

When she returned to St Helen's everybody had been especially kind of her. Sister Eliot had welcomed her with real warmth and old Mrs Smith had grinned toothlessly at her as if she was a long-lost friend.

It was two days after she went back to work before Claire realised that she had not seen Dr Duncan around. There was a new locum houseman with a hard face and a harder manner, and she did not contemplate, in her fragile state, asking after David from him. There was nobody else to ask and Sister Eliot simply told her that her 'young doctor' had gone and that this new one was 'as bad as the worst we've ever had'.

And Claire's life had eventually settled into the pattern which it still held. She had moved from the medical ward to the Renal Unit when there was room for her on the staff there, intending to eliminate renal nursing from her mental list of experience for the future. Instead she had found that she loved the work and the unit in spite of the sadness of saying goodbye to Sister Eliot and the ward where she had experienced some of the happiest and the most unhappy moments of her life.

Kidney failure seemed more and more to Claire to represent a really great challenge in nursing care. It was really a natural progression from the medical nursing which she had enjoyed so much, but, because the kidney transplant patients were nursed pre- and post-operatively on the unit, she found herself having to relearn a lot of surgical nursing skills too.

She attacked the new work with gusto and found herself forgetting, gradually, the daily sorrow of her bereavement. The meticulous observation, the total care of twelve ill patients and the challenge of keeping them emotionally adjusted to their chronic sickness, obliterated her personal unhappiness and provided a life-line for her.

She learned to see past the dialysis machines beside each bed and through the tangles of tubes to the little personal reminders of each patient's individuality which made the hospital home for them for the duration of their stay: the get-well cards, the flowers, the bright dressing-gowns and the small possessions that found a place on the locker tops.

Some of the patients, usually about half of those on the unit, were young, and many of these worked outside and came in once or twice a week for a night on the machine that cleaned their blood. They were a lively,

hopeful bunch who understood and helped in their own
care and brought a breath of fresh outside air into the
unit.

Their great hope was that they would reach the top of
the list for a kidney transplant and that one would
become available and they would have the operation
and be returned, as if by magic, to their former fit young
lives. It was a dramatic hope for a dramatic cure and
their faith in it filled Claire with wonder and admiration
for them.

Claire had been on the unit a year when Sister told her
that she was leaving to have a baby and that she wanted
Claire to apply for her job.

'I know you'll make a super job of it,' she said, 'and I
want the baby left in safe hands—if you know what I
mean.' They had got on well, both young and enthusi-
astic.

'I'll think about it,' Claire promised.

Claire had gone to lunch with a light heart for the first
time in weeks. It excited her that Sister thought her
ready and able for the taxing job. The opportunity of
running the Renal Unit seemed to set some seal on her
career for her. She decided she would try to get the job,
do it well, and perhaps climb the professional ladder at
St Helen's, the place that had sheltered her for so long.

Claire pushed her plate away and looked over at a
nearby table where a group of Sisters in their white
dresses and frilled caps sat eating and laughing with
some medical staff. It brought back happy memories of
her own lunches with David Duncan, and the unhappy
awareness that she had never seen him again.

The day she got the Sister's post, Claire made another
tremendous change in her life. She decided to move out
of the Nurses' Home. The decision might have had
something to do with Miss Humphreys—or Humph as
she was irreverently known behind her substantial back.

The Nursing Officer had sailed into the unit on the morning that Claire heard that she was to take it over.

'Congratulations, Staff,' she barked. The Renal Unit was her pride and joy, far more prestigious in her eyes than the other four wards over which she had administrative control. 'When are you leaving, Sister?'

Claire and the Sister looked at one another covertly, stifling their smiles. Humph was not known for her tact. They reminded her when Claire took over.

'Jolly good. Time to get used to the idea, eh, Staff? You'll need to sharpen up a bit for a Sister's post.'

'Er, yes, Miss Humphreys,' Claire said. She knew that the Nursing Officer thought her a shade too soft, mistaking her calm, gentle manner for lack of determination and authority. She would soon learn that this was not the case. Claire was not in the least worried by the remark. She had been nursing long enough to be undeterred by the Miss Humphreys of the profession.

'Now,' the older nurse was saying, 'why don't you come and have a cup of tea with me one of these evenings. I'm only four doors down from you on the same corridor in the Home, and I could perhaps give you a few hints . . .'

'But . . .' Claire began, and then stopped. Perhaps it wouldn't be wise to remind Miss Humphreys that she had lived four doors away for six months and the NO had never acknowledged her presence in the Home before. Claire had been mildly amused by the sheer feat of managing to ignore one's virtual neighbour for so long. She recognised the silent protest against having junior staff in the same part of the Home as Other Ranks.

'Thank you, Miss Humphreys,' Claire responded politely, 'perhaps I will, one day.'

'Fine, good girl,' Miss Humphreys said briskly. She

stormed out of the unit as disruptively as she had arrived, throwing glances like poisoned arrows from side
to side and terrifying staff and patients alike.

'Whew,' Claire said as she disappeared.

'You're in favour,' giggled Sister, 'tea for two eh?'

'It's joining the higher ranks that does it,' Claire
rejoined without rancour. 'I bet you got the same treatment and you're just not admitting to it.'

'Oh, no I didn't,' her colleague replied, 'I was safely
out in a flat by the time I got this post. It's living in that
does it. She thinks you've joined the ranks of the unmar-
riageable too . . .'

The remark was lightly made and without any hurt
intended, but to Claire it represented all the justification
she needed for moving out of hospital accommodation.
The thought had been there for ages, and she simply
hadn't bothered to do anything about it.

That evening she went straight to her little desk in her
room in the Nurses' Home and drafted the advertisement that she pinned on the notice board in the main
corridor of St Helen's the following day. Within a week
she had received a dozen answers, among them a neat
pencilled note:

'Would love you to consider sharing my little flat on
edge of park. I've just moved in, two bedrooms—one for
you. Rent reasonable.'

Fiona Shore was in a frantic state, working for her
final examinations. She said she knew there was a bit of
an age difference between them, but she did not have
any special friend in her own year—she had come into
nursing after a job in industry and felt more mature than
the other girls with whom she had trained.

The flat occupied the top floor of a Victorian terraced
house, like so many in the little streets that constituted
Elchester, and it was tiny and prettily decorated.
Claire's room overlooked the tree-lined street and,

beyond it, the park. She could walk to the hospital in fifteen minutes and into town in the same time. She moved in the following weekend.

In no time her room had taken on the feel that her bedroom at home had had, and she felt so much happier there than she had ever felt in the Home that she wished she had moved out long ago.

Fiona had passed her state finals and by now the flatmates were the best of friends. Fiona opted for theatre work as a staff nurse and within a year of passing her finals had landed the Sister's post on St Helen's busiest general operating theatre. The job, responsibility and drama suited her down to the ground and she soon had a reputation among the nurse learners for meticulous standards and strong, if modern, discipline in her theatre. When things got too much for her or a surgeon was particularly difficult she brought her troubles home to Claire whose greater experience was of invaluable help to her.

The other problems she brought home were boyfriend troubles and there were always plenty of those.

'Do you ever think about settling down, Claire?' Fiona asked her one evening after a long heart-to-heart over yet another of her own disastrous affairs.

'Not really. Why?'

'Well, you seem to be so marvellous about sorting out my problems, I'm sure you wouldn't make the dreadful mistakes that I seem to make,' Fiona answered.

'Oh, I probably would,' Claire uncurled herself from the depths of the armchair in which she had been sitting for an hour listening to Fiona. 'It's ne thing sorting out another person's problems and quite another avoiding your own,' she said. She hoped that she'd used a tone of voice that would put Fiona off asking any more questions. It had. 'I really love my job, you know,' she added, gently.

'Yes, I know you do,' Fiona answered, smiling at her friend.

But one way and another, it seemed that Claire could not escape the thought of marriage. Just when she thought she had done so and was settled deeply into her work in the unit, a staff nurse would tell her blushingly that she had got engaged over the weekend, or a student would ask her if she could possibly change the off-duty so that she could have a day off to go to a friend's wedding. Or Fiona brought her another story of disappointment followed by extravagant excitement over her latest conquest.

The seasons came and went and the park changed from its cloak of vibrant green to flower-filled summer and then donned rich autumn colours—she watched it change three times.

But at least she had the care and esteem of the nursing and medical staff of the unit, she reflected. And the new Registrar, Tony Fraser, had just asked her to go with him to the staff dinner in the Doctors' Residency.

Tony was tall and slim and easily flattered by professional praise, of which he received plenty from his medical superiors. Claire had respect for him professionally too, but she did not fancy him in the least. She had a shrewd suspicion that he had only asked her out because he could not be bothered to ask anybody else. He was fiercely ambitious and was regularly written off by new members of the nursing staff on the kidney unit as being uninterested in women and therefore not worth bothering with.

It amused Claire to hear the whispered news that yes, he was unmarried, and yes, he was more interested in a consultancy than a mortgage and the pattering of tiny feet.

And, in a serious, superior sort of way, Claire admitted that he was fairly attractive, although he was fast acquiring the arrogance of his elders, an attribute he presumably thought necessary for his promotion. Claire, after six months working with him, had decided that she could happily accept the odd invitation to hospital functions with Tony without tarnishing her reputation or being taken for granted. Such dates made a welcome diversion for her and did not affect the good working relationship that they enjoyed on the unit.

He'll end up on the shelf alongside me, she reflected, as she sat in the dentist's waiting-room, but for completely different reasons. By the time he's climbed the ladder high enough and thinks it's time he looked for a wife he'll find he's left it too late.

This thought was rudely interrupted by a gasp from the girl who was sitting in front of the bay window and who was now slipping slowly from it towards the floor. There were a few more people in the waiting-room by now, but none of them moved to help the fainting girl except Claire who found herself kneeling beside the figure slumped on the parquet flooring as if by instinct rather than by rational thought. She proceeded to act instinctively, loosening the clothing at the girl's neck and reaching for her wrist.

While she took the pulse, the girl's eyelids flickered open and then shut again and she mouthed her thanks to Claire.

'Just lie still and get your strength back,' Claire said softly. 'You'll be fine. You just passed out. Have you got a lot of pain still?'

The girl nodded.

Claire satisfied herself that the pulse was okay and decided that pain, plus the fact that the girl had probably not eaten that day in preparation for an anaesthetic had lowered her blood sugar. She was about to leave the girl to fetch a dentist to look at her when the door to the waiting-room opened and the blonde receptionist entered, accompanied by the tall stranger Claire had glimpsed earlier.

The man looked, not at the patient, but at Claire, with flinty grey eyes.

'Excuse me,' he snapped at her, and Claire moved out of range as he bent down and found the loosened clothing which Claire had got to first, and then the pulse which she had already taken.

'It's strong and regular,' Claire offered in a quiet, sure voice.

'I think I'm capable of ascertaining that for myself, thanks all the same . . .'

Claire took the full brunt of his bitter look while her mind registered that familiar Scottish lilt. The pallor, the thinness of his face and the signs of ageing around the hard eyes superimposed themselves on the remembered image she had kept so long. Yet she could not make the two images merge, they were so different.

She was almost certain that he must recognise her too and she waited for some clue, some reflection of his recognition to show in his eyes, hoping for a softening of that hard expression, even for the shy smile that she remembered. But nothing came.

Claire's heart turned over as he put his arms around the girl on the floor and lifted her effortlessly back onto her chair, where she slumped.

'You'll be all right, lassie,' he said. 'Nothing to eat this morning, I suppose? Damn silly.'

The man turned to the blonde behind him and smiled a smile at her in which his eyes played no part.

'Fine. Simple syncope, Miss Blackie. First aid hardly necessary,' he glared sarcastically at Claire.

'Thank you so very much, Dr Duncan,' said the receptionist sweetly, and Claire felt faint herself at the sound of that name.

So it is him and he's back in Elchester. Confused

thoughts chased themselves around her shocked brain.
But not at St Helen's surely?

She was almost glad when he followed the blonde out
of the waiting-room and even more glad, later, to have
her appointment over. She stopped in the shopping
centre and went automatically into the shop where she'd
seen the fruit bowl and bought it for Sue.

It was not until she was in the park that she allowed
herself to think, just for a fleeting moment, how her life
had been transformed by the new awareness of another
presence in Elchester.

CHAPTER TWO

WHEN Fiona burst into the sitting-room where Claire was reading in the early evening light, announcing, 'Guess what . . .' and 'You'll never guess what happened today. I couldn't believe it . . . I was furious,' Claire put down her book and prepared for the onslaught against some poor little butter-fingered student nurse.

'Well?' she said.

'Mr Matthewson only had one patient today,' Fiona gushed on, barely pausing to draw breath, 'and it was a little old lady with a long history of bowel trouble. He spent four hours resecting her and then this young upstart of a new registrar—first day in theatre with the chief—pipes up from where he's sitting next to the anaesthetist reading the casenotes, "I see she's eighty next birthday, sir . . ."

'Mr Matthewson looked up at him and said, "Yes a fine, fit old lady . . ." "For how much longer, sir?" says the Registrar. "Can we really justify operating on someone of her age? Perhaps she'd have lived perfectly happily until the end of her natural life without help from us, surgical help anyway."

'Thank goodness it was the end of the operation,' Fiona went on excitedly, 'Who does he think he is? Nobody, but *nobody* questions the chief's decisions to operate on his patients. Not even relatives.'

'Well, if she was very old, then perhaps the Registrar was right and perhaps the chief should be questioned,' Claire suggested, softly.

But Fiona was ready for this from her friend and her

faith in surgery was unshakeable—especially surgery undertaken by Harold Matthewson, her chief, all of which was unquestionably good for patients.

'Have you ever heard of quality of life rather than quantity?' Claire persisted.

'Oh, God, Claire. I can't argue with you about this sort of thing. Anyway, it isn't our worry. It's up to the doctors. Do you want a cup of tea?'

'Lovely, yes please. It's hard Fiona, but I sometimes have to help my patients to make the decision to live or die and it isn't easy to help them. But it is up to them really.'

'I don't know how you nurse those patients of yours. They all look so ill. At least I don't have to see how ill mine are. They're all draped and fast asleep by the time I see them,' Fiona gave her flatmate a wry smile.

Claire liked Fiona's self-honesty. She was a good and conscientious theatre sister and she did not kid herself about her personal ability to meet patients' emotional demands. Such integrity gave her another dimension beyond the superficial attractiveness of her pretty auburn hair and extraordinary turquoise-green eyes, and it was one quality which she had very much in common with Claire.

The telephone rang and Fiona answered it in the hall. She looked at herself in the mirror above the telephone table while she said, 'Yes, Sister Shore here. Yes, I'm on call. What is the case? Road-traffic accident, query ruptured spleen . . . okay, I'm on my way. Have you got the rest of the team in? And the student nurse, she lives in, what's her name? Yes, that's right. Have you sent a taxi for me? Fine.' The telephone settled back into silence. 'Poor old you,' Claire said, 'I'm just off to bed when I've read this chapter.'

'There's no need to be smug,' said Fiona, 'I'll have my

long weekend next week and anyway, I like a bit of
excitement. It might be the new registrar . . .'

The taxi sped Fiona through the quiet streets and up the
broad drive to the Casualty entrance of St Helen's. All
was light and bustle and subdued noise there. The
accident had clearly been a big one. There were two
groups of anxious relatives standing uneasily, talking in
little nervous outbursts which stopped as each new
victim was wheeled past them.

Several cars and a motorcycle had been involved in
the pile-up which had happened at a notorious road
junction a few yards from a blind corner marked by the
inevitable public house. The motorcycle had been
driven out of the pub car park and now the motorcyclist
was shouting abuse at those who were trying to see to his
injuries.

The sister on duty in Casualty came out from behind
some screens and greeted Fiona with a shrug over her
shoulder towards the patient.

'He's got nothing to shout about, poor bloke. Still, I
expect he'll be quiet enough by the time you get him.'

'He's for theatre is he?' Fiona asked.

'Yes, and a long job too, I'm afraid. Have you got time
for a cup of tea?'

'No, thanks, I don't think so. Got to be ready even if
they're slow seeing him down here.'

'Oh, there's nothing slow about the new surgical
registrar, is there?' Fiona caught a twinkle in the eye of
her colleague. Then, as if to dispel its effect, the Casualty Sister told her that the patient had already been seen
and was only to have another X-ray before being sent up
to theatre.

Armed with the certain knowledge that it would be
David Duncan who operated on this emergency, Fiona
prepared the theatre immediately as usual but with,

perhaps, just a shade more than even her usual care.

Nevertheless, the first words the surgeon uttered to her as the patient was wheeled into the operating area and they were scrubbing up side by side at the sink were bad omens for the future of their working life together. He glanced over to where the gown packs were lying half-open on the shelf and barked,

'Sister, is there any particular reason why you've put powder out for me rather than cream? I assume that you have heard of wound irritation traceable to the use of glove powder by surgical staff?'

'I certainly have, Dr Duncan,' Fiona replied with matching coolness, 'but Mr Matthewson always uses powder and his wounds never break down.'

'Sister, I don't give a damn whether or not Mr Matthewson's wounds break down. His operating techniques are different from mine. And I will use cream. Now.'

He glared at the first-year student nurse who had been called up for her first emergency in theatre and she scurried off, terrified, to find some glove cream for him. Fiona immediately called her back and then looked hard at Dr Duncan as she said to the girl,

'I'm sure the doctor meant to say please, Nurse. Thank you, Nurse.'

The student resumed her errand. 'Thank you, Sister,' she said as she made off.

The registrar stared furiously at the impassive, slim back of the theatre sister who continued to scrub her hands as if nothing had been said.

Fiona followed him, a few minutes later, into the theatre where she commenced a ritual check of everything that had been laid out for her by the junior nursing staff. They had been thorough. She found an abdominal pack half-opened and a splenectomy 'extra' pack ready, unopened, on a nearby shelf in case it was needed, along with a wide selection of sutures.

Fiona and the surgeon draped the patient, she handed him towel clips, and noted the strength of his long tapering fingers that looked as if they should belong to a pianist and not to a doctor. She glanced up once into his eyes above the green mask and they reflected the colour of the material around them, but beyond the reflection Fiona met ice-cold concentration on the task in hand.

He took the Hibitane swabs she offered him without looking at her face and swabbed the patient's skin at the operation site without apparently noticing the entry into the theatre of the young houseman. But when the assistant took his place at Dr Duncan's side, cap awry and obviously hastily clad in the chief's operating boots with his name vividly painted down their sides, the registrar eyed him and muttered something about hearing a bleep above the noise in a bar, then he turned to Fiona and asked her whether they could begin.

'Well, providing Sister doesn't have sabotage up her sleeve, we should be okay,' he said, having checked with the anaesthetist that all was well with his patient.

Fiona handed Dr Duncan a scalpel. She did not say anything. This rude man was not going to share a joke with her, especially not one at her expense. She had hoped for a happier atmosphere to offset the tension in the operating theatre during emergency surgery. She had even looked forward to work tonight. But now the case proceeded in tense silence.

It took three hours by the time the spleen had been removed and the abdomen thoroughly explored, but eventually the patient was ready to be taken to the recovery area under the charge of the student nurse while the rest of the team cleared theatre and the sister and surgeon took a cup of coffee. Fiona had mixed feelings about finding herself alone with Dr Duncan as the houseman rushed off to try to get a few precious hours in bed before he was called up again.

Dr Duncan was obviously pleased with the way the case had gone. He had made himself a cup of instant coffee by the time Fiona joined him in the surgeons' restroom and he had also helped himself to a biscuit from the tin. He was using his knees as a table, writing in the patient's casenotes '. . . skin closed with twenty interrupted 40 silk sutures. Rubber drain in situ . . .' when he glanced up coldly at the entrance of the theatre sister.

'For someone so keen on the relationship between the patient and the behaviour of the surgeon, you show remarkably little understanding of basic hygiene,' Fiona remarked. She made a mental note to tell Claire all about this man, her second brush with him having been no more satisfactory than the first.

He seemed supremely confident—over-confident even—and his arrogance offended Fiona and seemed to contaminate the neat, ordered theatre environment that she controlled so beautifully. She was determined to assert her authority and make it plain to him that she was mistress of her own domain.

The surgeon looked up and gave her a steady stare, 'What do you mean?' he asked, omitting to give her the basic courtesy of her title.

'I mean,' Fiona returned, 'that you should take your mask off when you come in here and not leave it hanging around your neck while you drink coffee.' She looked at where his mask lay crumpled where the dark stubble of his late-day beard began.

He followed her look with apparent interest. 'I had no idea how lucky we were,' he said levelly, 'to have a bacteriologist for a theatre sister.'

Fiona caught the full blow of his sarcasm and she reeled under it, while he saw and took immediate advantage of her momentary loss of poise. 'What a good thing she also knows how to make coffee.'

Fiona hoped, as she pulled her clothes on and undid the
knot of hair that had been hastily put up under her
theatre cap, that Claire had not gone to bed. It was after
one, but she longed to talk to her about tonight. Her
disappointment tasted bitter, like the last cup of coffee
she had swallowed so hastily.

Stepping out into the darkened corridor outside the
theatre suite, she blinked to accustom herself to the
comparative darkness of the night-time hospital, and
walked straight into Dr Duncan, a large, dark form
hurrying out of the men's changing-rooms next to the
door from which she had just emerged.

'Oh. I'm sorry,' she said automatically, stepping backwards away from the arm that threatened to break her
fall.

'Where do you live, Sister? I'll take you home,' the
registrar stated coolly.

'I share a flat, near the park, Monmouth Gardens,'
Fiona heard herself telling him.

He steered her down the surgical corridor and out of a
side exit from the hospital which took them out into the
dim car park outside the residency.

When she had seated herself in the front of his Rover,
Fiona found herself thanking him for his kind offer.
There were so few buses at that time of night, and the
walk did seem a little daunting after three hours on one's
feet.

'Quite so,' came the steely reply. 'Hundreds of flatmates are there?' Dr Duncan seemed almost bored by
the question he was asking.

'Only one, actually. She's completely different from
me,' Fiona smiled into the darkness, thinking what a
good story this would make for Claire after Dr Duncan
had dropped her at the flat tonight.

'How?'

'Oh, I don't know. She's more dedicated than me, I

think. Really a Florence Nightingale. She works all hours.'

'Where?'

'At St Helen's, of course,' replied Fiona, surprised at his direct questions. 'She's the sister on the Renal Unit, as a matter of fact.'

The hard lines of the profiled face beside her seemed to Fiona to set even harder, and her companion put his foot down hard on the accelerator so that they turned into Monmouth Street with a roar that would have awoken the stone lions in the park if that were possible. The Rover came to rest uneasily outside the flat.

'Would you like a cup of coffee?' Fiona asked. 'It was nice of you to bring me home,' she stated coolly, as if in explanation of her offer.

Dr Duncan turned off the ignition and followed Fiona up the narrow staircase to the flat, through the front door and across the tiny hall.

Claire had got engrossed in her book and had forgotten to go to bed. She was curled up in her favourite armchair, where Fiona had left her, still reading under the light of the standard lamp. The lamp cast a soft halo of light on her bronze hair and then over her face as she looked up at the sound of the front door.

Fiona stood in the sitting-room doorway with a tall, dark figure behind her, a disturbingly familiar figure to Claire's astonished eyes, and then she stepped into the room and said,

'Claire, let me introduce the new registrar in my theatre, Dr David Duncan. Dr Duncan this is Claire Brown, my flatmate. I'll just pop into the kitchen and put the kettle on for some coffee. Will you have some with us, Claire?' Fiona's look meant that she wanted Claire to stay for coffee.

With a supreme effort of will, Claire composed herself to cope with her second meeting with David Duncan that day. She stood up, swallowing to steady her voice before accepting, then she extended her hand formally to the surgeon.

'How do you do, Dr Duncan?'

'How do you do?' he returned coldly. 'We've met before. This afternoon,' he stated. 'Your flatmate has been telling me all about your talent for TLC.'

'I would have thought that tender loving care was a thing you needed for your job too,' Claire returned, 'in fact, I seem to remember . . .'

'Here we are then,' Fiona interrupted her, setting a tray down on the coffee table.

Claire took her coffee and drank it quickly. The hot liquid burned her throat, but hotter anger had begun to boil inside her. Why should she be the person to do the reminding? Why should she be humiliated by his rudeness and apparent unwillingness to admit to their past relationship? She would ignore it, and him, she decided.

As soon as she could gracefully leave them, Claire made an excuse and went to bed. But she found herself listening for the sound of the front door and hoping, against her will, that Dr Duncan would not prove to be another of Fiona's easy conquests.

The next morning the night nurses on the renal unit watched the calm approach of Sister Brown with relief. It had been a long night and they longed to get home to their beds. Claire had had a long night too, but for a different reason. She had had confused dreams when she had at last fallen asleep, the front door having clicked quietly open and shut again and the footsteps of Fiona disappeared behind her own bedroom door. She had awoken feeling still tired, and had walked through the park hoping that a hard day's work on the unit would dispel her confused feelings about Dr Duncan and clear her mind again.

She was just inside the unit door when the red alert

bell rang at the nurses' station and the two night nurses who had been standing there disappeared. Within a second, Claire and the night nurses were all clustered around the bed of one of the young patients, Alan Foster. He was sweating, pale and struggling for breath.

'Cardiac arrest,' Claire said, and she pushed the locker aside and began external cardiac massage. One of the more junior nurses had already rushed to get the 'crash' trolley and medical help, and this soon arrived in the form of Tony Fraser, the on-call anaesthetist, and junior medical support. The trolley they accompanied spouted wires, leads, recording paper and sundry other pieces of tubing attached to the vital equipment with it harboured, producing an impression of disarray which belied its carefully checked order.

The doors swung into action, dove-tailing their activity with that of the nurses who were already resuscitating the patient. The anaesthetist intubated the patient and began to breathe for him and Tony had, within seconds, applied ECG leads to his chest and begun to monitor his heart rate. Claire glanced up from what she was doing and noted with alarm the jerky, irregular trace which issued from the ECG machine.

Almost as soon as she had registered the thought, Tony Fraser voiced it:

'He's fibrillating. Let's shock him.' He put the two big black paddles of the cardioversion machine over the young man's heart and everybody stood clear of the bed with a single automatic response. The volts went through and all eyes turned back to the cardiograph machine. After a flicker the trace resumed its erratic pattern.

'And again,' Tony Fraser muttered as he repeated the shock to the patient's heart muscle. 'This should do the trick.'

Tony was almost as pale as his patient and beads of

sweat had gathered on his forehead and run down either side of his face and into his auburn sideburns. He was looking at the anaesthetist who was showing no sign of emotion, but checking and rechecking the patient's heart rate and breathing, running drugs into the vein he had cannulated in his arm, and synchronising his actions with those of Tony's.

As the second dose of volts went through, Alan Foster's heart gave a kick which leapt off the trace and Claire watched Tony holding his own breath, willing the patient back to life. After an endless moment the trace resumed normal rhythm and a tiny hint of colour returned to the patient's cheeks.

Claire returned Tony's gaze, she nodded imperceptibly as he said, softly,

'Got him.'

He was a good doctor, Claire thought.

An hour later Alan's cubicle had resumed some of its familiar order. He was reattached to his kidney machine and was propped up in a freshly made bed, managing to smile weakly at the remainder of the bustle around him. For the hundredth time, looking in at him, Claire wondered if he knew how close to death he had been, and for the hundredth time she could not decide. His demeanour suggested nothing of what might have happened inside his head during the last couple of hours.

At the nurses' station, Claire glanced at the clock. It was nine-thirty. The other patients had all been given their breakfasts and early morning medicines and baths while the drama surrounding Alan Foster had been going on. Claire called Sue over while the other nurses continued routine care.

'I'm afraid I'll have to ask you to special Alan today, Sue. Sorry—I know it's a miserable job for your last day. But I'd rather it was you, and I know he would too.'

Sue had kept up a bantering jollity whenever she was

in charge of Alan's care which Claire felt was postively therapeutic for the young man.

'I don't mind a bit, there's nobody I'd rather look after. It'll remind me why I want to come back to work after I get married!' Sue said, and Claire knew that she meant it.

At last the end of the afternoon arrived and Claire retreated to her room to prepare coffee, tea and sherry and to put out the cakes that the nurses had brought in for Sue's farewell party. Claire had decided not to make a speech at the presentation of the crystal fruit bowl. She didn't trust herself not to cry or make a fool of herself somehow. She felt very emotionally uncertain at the moment, and she was just worrying about this when Tony Fraser burst in.

'Hello, Claire. Where's the sherry? First to arrive, last to leave. That's me.'

'So I notice,' Claire said, relieved, smiling.

The following Saturday Claire ruminated upon her holiday plans as she walked to the Catholic Church in the town centre. The truth was, she didn't have any. She had spent every holiday since her parents had died either on courses connected with her work or with her ageing spinster aunts in Edinburgh. She supposed that she would visit them again soon, perhaps before Christmas, and then nurse on the unit over Christmas to give Sue a chance to spend it with her new husband.

It was a brilliantly sunny day and the church was fragrant with lilies and roses and small bunches of marguerites and freesia. The smell of white wax candles mingled with the flowers.

The wedding mass, which was in Latin, gave Claire time to wonder how, if she were standing up there before the huge altar, she would like the wedding to be. But she could not imagine herself beside the shadowy figure of the man in her imagination. She somehow just could not make it real for herself. I must really be destined for old-maidhood, she thought, as Sue, beautiful in white broderie anglais, stepped back down the aisle and passed her on the arm of her tall, handsome husband. Claire watched the bridesmaids, their cream dresses with coloured velvet sashes, swimming before her tear-filled eyes.

Sue had promised the patients that she would pop in to see them on the unit on her way to her honeymoon and she had persuaded Claire to come in too. Claire was happy to do this and was preparing to leave the reception to go to the unit and get organised before the newly-weds arrived when she caught sight of Sue and her husband moving towards the door themselves. There were cries of 'Good luck' and 'Take care of one another', and Claire stood up on tiptoe to see the couple. Seeing her, Sue grinned from the doorway and threw her bouquet of red roses so that they landed unmistakably at Claire's feet.

Embarrassed at all the amused looks she was getting from surrounding guests, Claire hurried to the door and made her way out into the sunny late afternoon, clutching the bouquet. What Sue had meant she could not imagine. Of all her acquaintances, Sue and Fiona were most aware of the lack of a man in Claire's life. Sue had even teased her about Tony the last time she'd been to a residency wine and cheese party with him, and Claire had told Sue firmly that theirs was definitely not a romantic liaison.

In her sitting-room on the unit, Claire stood with her back to the door, still confused and even a little angry with Sue for embarrassing her, arranging the offending bouquet in a vase. A sudden cold shiver down her spine made her aware that she was not alone, and she looked around expecting to see Sue and her new husband,

arrived for their triumphant tour of the unit. Instead the
doorway was filled with the bulky form of David Duncan.

He stepped silently into the room and Claire saw his
cold grey eyes take in her appearance from her glossy
hair to the brown sprigged dress she was wearing down
to her soft silvery-brown suede shoes. She felt the blood
leave her legs and rush upwards to burn her face, and she
still stood there, a red rose in her hand.

The distant memory of a similar situation flashed
painfully into her consciousness and she thought she
would faint if she did not sit down. She walked across to
her desk and faced him, leaning with one hand on the
desk top.

'Can I help you?' she heard herself ask as if it was
somebody else's voice that spoke the words.

She tried to look at him directly in spite of his steely
stare which seemed to cut into her.

'I didn't expect to find you still here at St Helen's after
all his time,' he said, his voice low.

The first intimate words that he had addressed to her
for more than five years sounded like swords.

'I . . . well . . . I . . .' Claire faltered and stopped.
How could she, *why* should she make excuses to him?
'Can I do anything for you?' she repeated.

'I thought this was the doctors' room,' Dr Duncan
informed her icily. 'Where is it?'

'Directly opposite, across the corridor,' Claire responded.

He gave her a look which might have had a suggestion
of confusion in it, or might have been plain dispassion,
turned and left the room, closing the door behind him.

Claire had time to register the fact that David Duncan
had not come to the unit expressly to find her, indeed
that he had obviously had an unpleasant surprise seeing
her there and that for some reason he was determined

not to renew their friendship, before Sue and her husband burst into the room.

It was much, much later, after they had gone, leaving the excited patients chattering with one another about how lovely Sue had looked in her red going-away outfit, that Claire was alone once more and she began to feel the new pain that he had left in her.

As she went out of the unit she waved to Alan Foster and put her head around his door when he beckoned to her.

'Didn't she look smashing?' he said of Sue.

'Smashing,' Claire agreed with a smile. 'And she'll be back in two weeks.' She knew how much Alan would miss Sue.

She would miss her too, Claire reflected as she crossed the bouncy, damp turf in front of the main gates of St Helen's. Perhaps she'd take a holiday herself when Sue got back. She felt terribly tired.

Claire had, as a young nurse, developed a habit of not looking at the beds occupied by patients whose deaths she feared, so as to protect herself from their deaths for as long as she could. Thus she would hurry from the ward door to the nurses' station when she went on duty, averting her eyes from the beds, and hearing the inevitable, dreaded truth from the nurse who was giving the report. This seemed to make it more bearable.

But as a Sister and an experienced nurse, Claire knew that she could not use this old ploy any more. She must face harsh truths squarely and help to make them bearable for her own juniors.

So it was that she noticed immediately, the next morning, the empty bed that had been Alan Foster's and was prepared for the unhappy face of the night nurse who was preparing to give her the report.

'Alan?' Claire asked, immediately she reached the station. The little night nurse's eyes were moist.

'Yes. He died at one o'clock this morning, Sister. There was nothing anyone could do. He arrested again,' she said in a soft voice.

'If only, if only . . .' Claire said, to herself, thinking of the hope that a transplant would have afforded him before he became too weakened by prolonged sessions on the kidney machine to cope with the operation.

'He was peaceful at the end,' the night nurse was saying.

'Good,' Claire responded. 'Did the relatives get there in time?'

'Yes, Sister. His parents were with him. They're coming back later this morning to do everything.'

'I'm glad he saw Staff Nurse Craig yesterday,' Claire said, 'he was especially fond of her.' She looked quietly at the night nurse and sat down to take the rest of the report. The nurses looked exhausted.

The day passed under the unnamed cloud of the previous night's death and although the nurses knew better than to refer to it, every one of the nurses on the two day shifts missed the young man in their own special way. Claire was glad when four o'clock came and she could disappear into her room for a final cup of coffee, change and get out of the hospital.

Tony knocked and came in while she was making her coffee and she made him some too. She was pleased to see him. He'd been out of the unit all day and the senior house officer who had been covering for him did not share Claire's total commitment to the patients as Tony did.

'Nice quiet day, Claire?' Tony inquired pleasantly, 'taking his coffee cup from her with a nod of acknowledgement. 'Everyone fine are they?'

'Yes. Were you with him too, Tony? Last night?'

Tony came over to her, put his cup down next to hers and laid a large warm hand on her shoulder. He looked down with frank blue eyes into her large brown troubled ones.

'It wasn't any good, Claire,' he said, 'he was never going to get well. He was too weak. It's a merciful release, that's all. I don't have to tell you that.'

'No. You don't. But thank you, Tony. It's most unprofessional of me isn't it? I really can't seem to help feeling like this at the moment. And I think I'm getting worse.' Claire resisted the almost irresistible pressure of unwanted tears behind her lids. This was stupid, she thought. What was happening to her?

'I know, Claire . . .' Tony's voice was unexpectedly soft and concerned. He was looking at the vase of red roses which glowed in the afternoon sunshine by the window. He bent towards them, inhaling their scent and then he said in a gentle voice,

'Claire, isn't it time you took a holiday? I mean, I know it's none of my business, but I can't remember the last time you had a decent break away from the unit . . .'

'Yes,' Claire responded uncertainly. 'I was wondering whether I might take a holiday, actually . . .'

She was astonished by this sudden expression of personal interest in her by the registrar. It was strange that she knew so much about him professionally and so very little personally. He had always been only superficially interested in her feelings, her ideas and her personal life—in fact he had shown no real interest at all and she had been happy keeping their relationship on the level of unit gossip. Now, suddenly, Tony was speaking to her with genuine interest and concern.

There was a slight frown on his forehead and a new softness in the blue eyes that she knew so well. He stooped towards her slightly, holding his cup in one hand, the other buried deeply in the pocket of his white coat from which escaped the inevitable head of a coiled stethoscope. His curly auburn hair sprang back from his

high forehead, accentuating his height, and there
seemed to be a new intensity about him that Claire did
not recognise.

'Actually,' she said, to break the strange silence that
had fallen over them, 'I was thinking of taking a couple
of weeks after Sue gets back from her honeymoon.' She
thought seriously for the first time about the possibility.
'Perhaps I'll go walking in the Lakes for a week or two.'

'What a good idea. Lovely and restful. Just the job.
Look here . . .' Tony Fraser replaced his hands on
Claire's shoulders and held her firmly, facing him, 'I
need a break too,' he said, 'I know this might sound a bit
odd of me to suggest it, but well, why don't we go
together?'

Claire looked at him, amazed at the idea, taken
off-guard by it.

'We could go up in my car,' he continued, 'walk and
talk. No ulterior motive.' He smiled and Claire returned
the smile.

'Well, it would be rather nice to have some company,'
she heard herself saying uncertainly.

'Even if it's a bit in the nature of a busman's holiday?'
Tony grinned back, his hands dropping to his sides as if
their work were completed.

'We wouldn't have to talk shop all the time,' Claire
said.

Tony pushed his hands down into his pockets again
and stood up.

'It's a deal then,' he said. 'Now go home and sleep well
tonight. Don't take your work off duty with you. You
should know better than that.'

'I certainly should by now,' Claire said, 'but thank you
for reminding me, Tony.'

The name sounded different to her now, associated as
it was with the thought of shared time ahead out of the
familiar routines and environment of St Helen's.

Claire was surprised at herself for agreeing so readily to Tony's plan. But it was as if fate had taken a hand and there was nothing that she could do to change course. She began to think about the holiday with a strange mixture of excitement and anxiety.

'See you tomorrow, then,' Tony said, at the door of her room.

'Yes,' she said, 'fine.'

Friends, she thought, as she walked home in the early evening sun, appear in the most unexpected ways sometimes.

CHAPTER THREE

THE list was going badly. Mr Matthewson, Consultant Surgeon, washed his hands with contemptuous care. He did not speak, but his gaze, when it lighted upon another member of the team, was icy.

Somehow they had got through two cases this morning and both had been complicated. The anaesthetist was a duty officer, a locum, not known to Mr Matthewson and this fact did not improve the mood of the chief. The late summer sun beat in through the windows of the theatre suite on the fifth floor of St Helen's surgical block and it was ferocious. Everything the surgical team touched seemed to be on fire and the five minute air change—so efficient as an aid to sterility—seemed to be pumping the same tropical heat around the masked and gowned figures.

The first patient, a young appendicitis case who had not even been an emergency, but a 'cold' case, had bled. Mr Matthewson had spent two intense hours over a job that should have taken forty minutes and been delegated to a junior. He had therefore missed his coffee break with ill-disguised disgust. Normally the new registrar, David Duncan, would have supervised the young house-man and used the case of appendicitis as a teaching case, the danger of peritonitis being remote—a rare thing in a surgical case which was normally presented as an acute emergency.

Instead, David had 'phoned in to say he wouldn't be coming to theatre until a quarter of an hour before the first case was due to begin. This had left the chief fuming silently and taking the case with only Sister and a houseman to help him, torn between his fury at being let down at such unreasonably short notice and his professional and personal loyalty to his young protégé.

Fiona had taken the brunt of his rage. He had not exactly attacked her, but he had attacked everybody else through her, so that by the time the second case had arrived on the operating theatre table, she had been close to tears as a result of his barbed remarks.

The gall bladder removal had also been complicated and had taken longer than it should have done and when coffee time at last arrived, Fiona had spent most of it in the changing room comforting the student nurse, Jarvis, who had been yelled at by the chief for tying his gown too tightly, stepping in a disposal skip and handing Fiona the wrong suture three times.

'Bad morning we're having,' Mr Matthewson commented to Fiona, not too unpleasantly, over the second belated skin closure.

'Yes, sir,' she answered miserably.

'What's up with Dr Duncan, anyway? Give you any clue when you spoke to him?'

'No, sir. It wasn't him actually. It was a friend who 'phoned for him. Another doctor by the sound of him. He didn't give me any details at all. Just said he'd be in touch himself soon.'

'He'll probably ring me later today,' the chief mumbled. 'If later today ever arrives, that is . . .'

Fiona took his twisted smile and returned a sweet one of her own, then watched him striding off, removing his gown as he went, and heard him booming at the houseman in the restroom. There were times, Fiona felt, when she was glad not to be a junior doctor. Senior medical staff spared the nurses more often than not—probably for all the wrong reasons, Fiona smiled to herself—and vented all their real rage on their inferiors in their own profession.

Her mind slipped back over the three weeks that Dr David Duncan had been Surgical Registrar. He had started off arguing with and finished up the blue-eyed boy of Mr Matthewson. It was a remarkable achievement. More than she had managed with the registrar, Fiona thought ruefully. If she had entertained any romantic hopes in that direction she had been over-optimistic, she now knew.

Dr Duncan had not made any real effort to conceal his indifference towards her, ever since the evening of the emergency when he had taken her home. He treated her with cool deference in the theatre but often she might as well have not been there as far as communication with her directly went. He worked fast, efficiently and calmly and was even patient with Nurse Jarvis, a feat unmanaged by any other member of the medical staff.

The only times when Dr Duncan went out of his way to speak to Fiona seemed to be in a very strange connection: that of Claire.

Several times the registrar had asked after Fiona's flatmate in what seemed to her to be a rude and sarcastic manner and then, yesterday, he had stunned her by referring to Claire's holiday. Fiona could not imagine how he knew that Claire was planning a holiday in the Lake District with the Renal Unit Registrar, or what business it was of his anyway. So she had been shocked when Dr Duncan had come over to her in a quiet moment in the restroom and asked her how she felt about her 'Florence Nightingale friend going off on holiday with a man'.

'But she and Tony are just good friends,' Fiona had flung the cliché at him furiously. How dare he be so personal about her flatmate, she asked, forgetting who he was or the usual formalities in the heat of her anger on her friend's behalf.

To her further surprise, Dr Duncan appeared to

recognise that he had overstepped some mark, and had actually apologised in a stumbling sort of a fashion and had followed the mumbled 'sorry, I shouldn't have said that', with an invitation to join him for a drink later that week.

Fiona had felt an odd response of mild outrage and delight at his actually asking her out after days and days of bleak semi-communication, and she had gone home and told Claire of the exchange with the registrar.

Claire had been just as surprised as Fiona at the registrar's remarks about the holiday.

'How on earth did he know?' she asked her friend, who was at a loss to reply.

'Anyway, I won't have him being rude about you to me, why or how or where doesn't matter. Especially if I'm going to see him off-duty.' Fiona allowed herself to smile for the first time during this conversation.

Claire stopped packing. The article of clothing she had been folding had fallen crumpled into the suitcase.

'Off-duty?' she asked, unable to hide her shock.

'Yes,' Fiona said, chirpily, apparently unaware of it, 'he's asked me out for a drink next week.'

And now fate had intervened and Dr Duncan had gone off sick for an unknown period of time and he hadn't bothered to contact her. It was just as if he had never made the leap across their working relationship and asked her out for that drink.

She might as well forget it, she thought, and go out with the registrar from Orthopaedics who had been pestering her for six months to accompany him to endless changes of film at the local flea-pit in Elchester. At least he was fun, Fiona thought, which was a great deal more than Dr Duncan was proving to be.

The morning rose mistily over Ambleside. In the cheerful dining-room of their small hotel, Claire and Tony planned their day and ate their breakfast of scrambled eggs, bacon, toast and tea. Breakfast had never tasted so good to Claire. After nine hours of solid sleep she had recuperated after the long drive up in Tony's old and inelegant car, and now she looked forward to a day in the hills.

Tony had been good company so far. He had been as good natured as he so often was at work when the pressure was not too great for chatting with patients and staff. He hadn't talked shop too much and they had chatted about trivialities all the way here. Now she was beginning to relax and to feel as if she was really on holiday.

'Does ten miles sound too much to you?' Tony was asking her now, looking up from his map.

'I don't think so,' she replied, 'although I'm a bit rusty. I think I'll manage that, though. Shall I ask for a packed lunch?'

The hotel did excellent packed sandwich lunches for walkers, and now, at the end of the season, they were even better than usual, the landlady having plenty of time to prepare them for the dwindling number of guests. There was a relaxed air about the little hotel. The landlady and her husband seemed to be being extra kind to her and the place felt even more welcoming than it had before. The management knew Claire well for she had been there for many years with her mother and father. Although obviously mildly surprised to find her turning up with a young man, they now behaved as if the inevitable had happened and the 'nice young nursing sister' had got herself a nice young man at last.

'He's not a real boyfriend, you know,' the landlady told her husband discreetly after the bar had closed the night before, 'they're in different rooms don't forget. It's a pleasant change to find young people behaving decently,' she told him.

Claire found that she had laid some ghosts by coming to the hotel with someone else. For the first time since her parents had died she felt at ease there. She had so often sat in this dining-room and envied other young people, always in couples, sometimes obviously honeymooning, at the other tables.

She looked much younger than her twenty-six years though. When she went upstairs to change, Claire tied her thick, burnished hair back with a red spotted headsquare tied gipsy-fashion, tucked her close-fitting brown needlecord trousers into her long red walking socks, and tied her boots carefully before straightening up and surveying her slim, well-proportioned form in the mirror critically. Nursing had one big compensation, she reflected, it left you little time for over-eating.

She was glad she had agreed to come on holiday with Tony. All worries, misgivings and disturbing preoccupations had been replaced by a sense of pleasant anticipation of the days that lay ahead and, noting the lights in her eyes, Claire smiled at herself in the mirror before going down to meet Tony in the hall of the hotel. He greeted her approach with an appreciative look and a mock whistle of approval.

As they passed through the centre of the little town to get out on to the crags, a market was getting underway. Stalls were already selling vegetables and fruit to local housewives and Claire stopped and purchased a pound of Cox's apples.

The cool morning air was exhilarating and they made their way quickly out of town and up a winding flint track that branched off the road. Climbing up through a sparse coppice of larch and ash, they inhaled the scent of moss and the musty smell of the fungi which crouched at the bases of winter-wet trees.

Within an hour of steady climbing, Claire and Tony had reached a vantage point from which they looked down at the cluster of houses that marked the outskirts of Ambleside. They had emerged from the trees into a bright, sunny, clear sky-blue day and nobody else was in sight. The world was silent but for the sound of a stream which rushed down to the right of their path.

'So much life,' Tony said softly. He was standing very close to Claire beside the water. She could not decide whether her breathlessness was due to the climb or to a sense of unease about what Tony was going to say.

'Life?' she questioned him.

'Can't you see them?'

'What?'

'The tiny trout.' Tony pointed and Claire followed his direction with a sudden relief of the tension she had felt building up in her.

'I can't see anything,' she almost laughed.

'Hundreds,' Tony insisted. He put his arm around her and pointed again so that her face was close to his as they looked together.

Suddenly she could see the tiny fish and she pulled away saying, 'Ah yes. Aren't they well camouflaged? You can hardly see them.'

'Yes. Like nurses,' Tony answered, giving her a direct look. 'You can't see that they are really women in their natural habitat—the hospital.'

'No, I suppose you can't,' Claire said. She moved quickly away from him and continued up the path.

He said nothing more but caught up with her and they walked on upwards in silence. Claire, although annoyed that Tony had broken their mood of easy companionship, felt well able to cope with his advances if they remained as indirect as that one had been.

Gradually, their easiness together was restored and when they stopped for lunch Tony took a waterproof and spread it on the ground for them to sit on while they ate their picnic. Claire unpacked sandwiches, fruit and a flask of welcome hot coffee and they sank down gratefully in the lee of a rock to eat, their hands cupped round their hot drinks.

Beneath them the valley spread away in three directions and the land rose again in grey peaks from their green fields. The sky heaped itself over the mountains in layers of white moving cloud and the wind rushed across the path that they had just climbed, enveloping them for a moment in a swirling white mist.

Claire felt Tony move almost instinctively towards her, but he did not put an arm around her as she feared that he might. In a minute the mist cleared and they were in sunshine again, both chilled and with drops of moisture on their eyelids and lashes where the mist had condensed on them.

As they set off again, Claire broke the silence between them. Pointing down the peak she remarked,

'How dreadful not to be here to see this.' She felt that the beauty around them outweighed anything that might have worried her under other circumstances and she was determined to keep her friendship with Tony open, in spite of his apparent changing attitude towards her.

'Yes. I know what you mean,' he said, looking down too.

'I wonder whether Alan Foster ever came here, ever walked like this in the autumn and saw these colours,' she continued dreamily.

'I don't know. Poor guy. We certainly tried for him.'

'Yes,' Claire slowly began to walk on down the path.

'He needed a transplant,' Tony went on matter-of-factly.

Claire stopped and looked round at Tony, surprised. 'I didn't even know he'd been considered for a transplant,' she said, 'I thought he was too ill right from the time he was first referred to us.'

'No. Not exactly. There was never a suitable donor.

Rare tissue type and no family young enough to take the risk of giving him a kidney.'

'How often does that happen? I mean, I know how hard it is for us to get donor kidneys from accident victims and so on. But how often do people die because there is nobody alive or dead to give them a transplant?'

'Very often,' Tony said. 'We're working with the research boys on tissue typing techniques that will give us a chance of improving the success rate of transplants of kidneys from live donors. At the moment the best results are with transplants between identical twins. We've got to improve on that and there isn't any reason why we shouldn't stumble on a key factor in tissue typing. Trouble is, we need guinea-pigs—human ones. We've done the tests on one another—the medical staff—and they're very simple. But we don't feel like advertising for volunteers on such an emotionally charged project as this.'

'But it isn't dangerous to have the tests, is it?'

'No, not at all. Just a matter of being prepared to have them repeated if something goes wrong in the lab.'

'You've never asked me,' said Claire.

'No. We decided against asking for the nursing staff's help. For some reason it's vaguely insulting to be asked to be a guinea-pig. Don't know why.' Tony grinned at Claire, but she was serious-faced.

'As soon as we get back I want you to test me,' she said. She was haunted by the thought of Alan Foster brave in his lonely illness.

'A fit person can get on perfectly well with only one kidney,' he said, 'Nature was kind and gave us two of most things and we can often manage quite well with one.'

'I'd give one of my kidneys away—if the cause was good enough,' she ventured lightly.

'Not if I have anything to do with it you won't,' Tony

replied just as lightly. 'We need a whole Sister on the unit, not half of one.'

'That's all you're interested in, isn't it, Tony Fraser? You and your unit . . .'

Claire realised too late what she had laid herself open to, and sure enough Tony had turned to face her, blocking her way on the narrow path.

'No,' he said, fiercely, 'the unit is not all I'm interested in, Claire, although I think you would prefer that it was.'

'I'm sorry, Tony,' Claire said, meekly, 'I didn't mean to upset you.'

They walked on, passing a group of sleepy sheep who blinked at them, each bulky form seeming immune to the bitter wind.

'We have to be so careful not to lead the public into accepting new technology that isn't absolutely proven, haven't we?' she inquired of her silent companion, changing the subject on to neutral territory again.

'Well, we could wait forever if we waited for them to trust us completely,' he said in a normal voice. 'Look at how long it's taken for corneal grafting to become trusted. We've been doing that since the thirties in this country, and kidney transplants for almost as long and we still can't get enough donors. I'm just glad I chose renal surgery and not hearts.'

Claire did not answer, the memory of the effect of her last comment was still all too fresh in her mind, but she thought how typical Tony's remark was of this ambitious young doctor. Sometimes, she thought, she despaired of her medical colleagues.

The last of the sun filtered through the autumn trees and beneath their feet the floor of the wood was soft and moist. The blood pulsed around Claire's body and she felt healthier than she had done for a long time. The two walked down to the road and approached the town again. As the hotel came into sight, Claire sighed and said,

'I'm going to have a long, deep bath. And then I'm going to change. And then I'm going to meet you in the bar and buy you a before-dinner drink to thank you for a lovely day.'

'Well, Sister,' Tony replied with a smile, 'that sounds just great.'

An hour and a half later Claire came into the softly-lit bar in a cream silk shirt and slightly dark toned skirt, moving gracefully between the tables to where Tony sat. He looked up from the local evening paper.

'Very smart,' he said.

'Thank you,' Claire responded simply.

To the right of the table they chose for dinner later, a huge pot of tawny chrysanthemums and copper beech leaves stood upon the wooden dresser, contrasting vividly with the cool blue and white willow pattern plates ranged above it. Beside the vase, glasses of fruit juice and bowls of fresh fruit salad stood waiting for the diners.

'It looks like harvest festival in the church where I used to go as a child,' Claire said.

Tony did not answer but remained withdrawn during their first and second courses and Claire continued to make small talk, nervous of what he might be thinking after his few words spoken on the hillside this afternoon. Her misgivings were confirmed when, as they waited for their cheese to be brought to them, Tony leaned across the table and took her hand.

'Claire. How do you feel about me?' he asked her.

'I like you very much,' Claire responded truthfully. She could not bring herself to withdraw her hand from his.

'I've been wanting to ask you to come out with me properly. I mean out of the hospital, but you always seem so busy and . . .'

'No, Tony,' Claire interrupted him, 'Our friendship isn't that kind . . .'

'But, it could be so different . . .'

'No, Tony. Don't make me be unkind to you . . .'

Tony took his hand away and looked up ungratefully as the landlady put their cheese down in front of them. 'Would you like some more butter, sir?' she asked and Tony refused it curtly.

They finished their meal in uneasy silence and Tony adjourned to the bar with his coffee while Claire made an excuse and went to her room.

When she got there she sat down on the bed and thought angrily about the events of the day. Just what she had not wanted to happen had happened and she placed the blame fairly and squarely on Tony's shoulders. He had promised her 'no ulterior motive' to the holiday and right from the beginning he had broken his own rules. She had not led him to expect anything from her and it was up to him to sort out his ideas and to apologise to her, she decided.

She did not want a romantic liaison with Tony Fraser, of that she was sure. He was not bad-looking. He was kind. He understood her work. But there was something missing and it was something that she had briefly known with someone else and would never be able to do without again.

Claire felt that Tony's clumsy approaches towards her were calculated for their convenience and that if it had not suited him to find a girlfriend on his own doorstep he would not have paid her a moment's attention.

She undressed slowly and got into bed between the crisp white sheets. She put on the bedside lamp and opened her book. She decided before she began to read that she would wait to see Tony's behaviour at breakfast the next morning. If he behaved normally she would say nothing and the holiday could go on as planned, but if she detected any bad atmosphere or resentment in him she would simply catch the next train home. It was as simple as that.

But Tony was evidently not going to bear malice. He was sitting happily at their table beside the autumnal flower display the next morning when Claire came down, rather hesitantly, for breakfast. She was dressed in a skirt and jersey, prepared to bring the holiday to a premature close if Tony's behaviour warranted it, and Tony took in her appearance immediately.

'A skirt?' he asked with surprise in his voice and on his face, 'aren't we walking today then?'

'Well, I didn't know . . .' Claire sat down, relieved that Tony was so genuinely disappointed.

'Oh, Claire, I haven't disgraced myself that badly, have I?' he looked her straight in the face. 'I can take a rejection, you know. I'm not a baby.'

'I'm not very used to having to hand them out,' Claire admitted frankly, sorry for Tony but terribly glad at the same time that she had found the strength to tell him honestly how she felt about him.

'I could see that,' Tony smiled wryly. 'But I can't believe you've led such a sheltered life. What do you do with yourself all those evenings when your fast flatmate is out on the town?'

The question caught Claire so unawares that she dropped her knife. Tony retrieved it for her and handed it back calmly, looking quizzically at her as if amused by her amazement.

'What do you mean?' she asked.

'You know perfectly well what I mean. Old fast Fiona the Heartless', Tony grinned openly, pleased with his own wit.

'I didn't know you knew her,' Claire replied coldly.

'I don't. Her latest conquest is a very old friend of

mine. That's all. I'm not slandering your friend. Forget it.'

Claire thought she could detect a suggestion of irritation in Tony's voice. 'Anyway, I don't think Fiona has been particularly heartless. At least not with *him*.'

'Oh. Don't you? Well, she's not had a lot of time yet, has she?'

'Anyway,' Claire heard herself saying, 'I should think they're fairly perfect for one another.'

The thought of David Duncan and Fiona together made her feel cold and faint, so she sat up straight in her chair and readjusted her hold on the present, the warm breakfast-room and the bustling reality of the street outside the window, full of early morning shoppers.

'You don't know him like I do. She's not the woman for him,' Tony rejoined firmly, and the conversation was obviously closed from his point of view.

It was not until that evening, after a lovely day out in the hills with no untoward remarks or encounters to disturb Claire's enjoyment of the day, that she realised that they had not made clear between them who Fiona's new boyfriend was. She had just assumed . . . She decided to broach the subject anew after they had finished their meal and were sitting together in the cosy bar, drinking their coffee.

'We are talking about the same person, aren't we. Fiona's new boyfriend, I mean,' Claire ventured. Tony stopped mid-reach as he leaned towards the magazine rack to pick up a copy of *Horse and Hound*.

'Probably,' he said casually, 'I'm sure she'll have lured him back to the flat by now. David Duncan. New Surgical Registrar on her theatre suite.'

Claire felt the blood rush to her face as she heard his name spoken.

'You sound jealous!' she said to Tony to cover her confusion.

'Huh!' was all the response that this remark met with.

'Not new to St Helen's . . .' Claire began, and before she could regain control over the conversation she had let Tony know unmistakably that she knew David Duncan. It was his turn to be amazed.

'But he hasn't been at St Helen's for years,' he said.

'Five years,' Claire corrected softly, 'In fact, I hardly recognise . . . recognised him.' She looked down into her lap. 'And he certainly doesn't recognise me.'

Tony was staring at her with a mixture of surprise and care, as if he knew more than he could possibly know.

'Perhaps he didn't want to recognise you,' he told her gently. 'He's . . . well, he's not a very well man.'

Claire felt her stomach turn over. 'What do you mean?' she asked.

'David and I were at university together,' Tony began in a low voice, 'or, at least, when I went up to university David was already there, trying to pass his first-year exams for the third time. It wasn't that he was stupid, he was ill. He passed the re-sits and then seemed to be fitter for quite a while. Then he went off sick again and then returned, and that was the pattern of his student life. He worked like hell, much harder than any of the rest of us, and came to parties and lived a fairly normal life until his final year. He was off for the first half of it, and then he came back and just worked solidly, never went out, and passed his finals, winning the gold medal for our year on the way. He had turned himself into a brilliant clinician. He was a natural doctor. You could feel that he belonged on the ward, with patients.'

'He chose medicine for his first house-job,' Claire's mind flew back to her memories which she kept locked away so carefully and she fought the tears that threatened to fall into her coffee.

'Then he became sick again,' Tony was saying. 'It seemed to be a battle that he just couldn't win, and the next time he returned it was only for a brief time as an in-patient before he left and spent a while doing a sick children's course. Over the next few years I watched him change. As he continued to be ill it was as if he lost his faith in medicine . . '

Tony broke off, suddenly aware of Claire again, as if he had been talking to himself.

'But what was wrong with him?' Claire asked, her overwhelming concern banishing discretion.

'*Is* wrong, you mean . . . Oh, God Claire, I shouldn't talk about it behind his back. It's just that if it hadn't been for David I don't think I would ever have qualified. He was such an example . . .'

'Yes,' said Claire, 'I can imagine.' It was her turn to be gentle with Tony.

'And don't worry, Tony, I won't breathe a word of this to Fiona. I know you feel guilty about telling me.'

'Thanks,' he said, 'but I expect she'll know by now. He 'phoned me the night before we came up here and told me he wanted me to come and see him. I went and I told him I felt he needed more dialysis and that he must face up to facts and stop work for a while again. So I'm certain he missed the next morning's list.'

'Dialysis.' The word rang hollowly around Claire's brain. Renal failure! She could hardly believe her ears or the remorseless calculations that were going on in her mind. So, David Duncan was dying, as surely as Alan Foster had been dying.

They both finished their coffee in silence, then Tony broke it by saying, 'Look, Claire. On a happier subject, I know I was hasty when we first got here and that you were angry with me—but I would like to get something cleared up before we get back on the treadmill at St Helen's, and so that we understand one another for the rest of the holiday. I . . .'

Claire listened quietly, numbly, while Tony continued, 'I don't want to rush you into anything you don't want in terms of a relationship, but I do need a partner for hospital functions and my work doesn't leave too much time for socialising outside the hospital, as you well know. What I'm trying to say is, please, will you agree to come out with me from time to time, perhaps slightly more often than we used to? I won't rush you, I promise.'

Tony was looking straight into her eyes and Claire felt a rush of liking for him. The discovery of a mutual, if secret, concern drew her to Tony.

'Yes, Tony, of course I will,' she told him. He leaned across and gave her a quick light kiss on her cheek and Claire was surprised by the warm feeling it left on her face.

'Tony,' she said, 'thank you for everything.'

Fiona was woken by the telephone, although she was not on call and it was her day off.

David Duncan's voice was deep and serious.

'I believe we missed our date at the end of last week, Sister Shore,' he said. 'Are you free this evening?'

'I'm washing my hair,' Fiona told him, not without sarcasm.

'I was afraid you might be,' came the unmoved voice, 'or else that you might have had a date with Paul Newman.' The remark was humourless.

'All right, Dr Duncan, where shall I meet you?' Fiona could bear it no longer.

'I'll pick you up around eight.'

Fiona felt that her playing it cool had paid off in the end. She decided not to lounge in bed, but to get out and buy herself a new dress and even, perhaps, some shoes too. She skipped into the bedroom, holding her kaftan around her, and then into the bathroom where she ran herself a long and luxurious bath.

As she lay soaking in it she looked forward to seeing her flatmate again and exchanging news. Claire would be home tomorrow. Fiona was full of curiosity about Claire's relationship with Tony Fraser. He was quite good-looking in a studious sort of aloof way. And now she would have news for Fiona too. She wondered what it would be like to sit over a drink with David Duncan. He had certainly taken his time over asking her out.

She put on a pair of black trousers and a soft black velvet top that evening. She had not found a dress that pleased her in the shops and she was putting on an old outfit that Claire admired on her. Fiona had never managed to boost Claire's confidence enough for her to borrow the black top and trousers, and the thought made Fiona smile now, in sadness rather than in amusement.

But confidence, Fiona soon realised, was not a commodity much admired by her companion of this evening. He had turned up on the dot of eight o'clock and had ushered her briskly into the Rover and driven her just as briskly out of Elchester—without a word. Then, as he took her coat politely and hung it on the antique coat stand in the corner of the tiny bar he had brought her to, he glanced coolly at her.

'You needn't have gone to the trouble of dressing up. This place is quite an ordinary little local.'

'And so it was,' Fiona told Claire the following day. 'So much for a romantic night out . . .' she looked aggrieved at Claire.

'What happened?' Claire asked.

'What didn't happen, you mean,' Fiona grimaced. 'I sat at this old wooden table while he went up to get us drinks and the crowd of locals at the bar turned round and ogled at me. I felt terrible, so overdressed and out of place, and Dr Duncan didn't bat an eyelid. I might as well have been wearing a sack as far as he was concerned. In fact, he looked as if he'd have preferred it if I had. I should have known better than to go out with him at all. I knew how self-opinionated and unpredictable he was before I went . . .'

'Have you been out with him much?' Claire ventured.

'Certainly not,' her flatmate answered. 'If that was the off-duty Dr Duncan, I think I'll stick to the on-duty one from now on. Which reminds me,' Fiona picked an orange from the fruit bowl on the table between them and held it between both hands as if it were a crystal ball, then stared into it thoughtfully, 'he asked me when you were back on duty after your holiday.'

'Me?' Claire exclaimed.

'Yes. And he made one or two very scathing remarks about your going on holiday with Tony Fraser. And,' she waited a second, 'he asked me whether you were involved with Fraser.'

'Why doesn't he ask me himself if he wants to know?' Claire burst out with uncharacteristic lack of control.

'Good question,' Fiona said, 'I'll ask him for you if you like.'

'Don't you dare,' Claire quickly said, grinning at her friend.

'How *did* you get on with Tony Fraser?' Fiona persisted mischievously, 'Did he behave?'

'Mostly,' Claire said, truthfully. 'We had a lovely time.'

'So you keep saying.'

'Anyway, I found out how Dr Duncan knew that I was going on holiday with Tony Fraser: they used to be at university together. They're very old friends.'

'Really?' Fiona lifted her eyebrows.

'Well, he's certainly concerned that your relationship with the famous Dr Fraser isn't too deep and, if you ask me, I think he's quite interested in you.'

'Me?' Claire exclaimed.

'Yes, you. He must have fallen under your spell over the coffee mugs that evening he brought me back to the flat after that emergency case. He is definitely not interested in me.'

'But he's not interested in me,' Claire insisted, uncomfortably aware that she was hiding from Fiona, 'he pretends I don't exist. He ignores my presence.'

'Well, if you must be convinced, I got the definite impression that the only reason he took me out at all was to find out about you. He kept asking about you . . .'

'I don't think Dr Duncan sounds like a very nice person any more . . .'

Fiona jumped in at this slip. 'Any more?'

'I mean,' said Claire, 'from what you say, he doesn't sound a very nice person,' she finished carefully.

Fiona cast her an old-fashioned look, but did not pursue the conversation further. Claire, in her own comfortable bed later that night, did not pursue it either. She tried to push it from her mind, and went to sleep thinking about the fresh colours of the Lakeland hills and the gentle pools in which her own and Tony Fraser's reflections had fallen, side by side, for two happy weeks.

CHAPTER FOUR

CLAIRE was only slightly upset by the cool attitude adopted towards her by Tony when they returned to work after their holiday. She had expected him to replace their relationship firmly on a professional footing and, if he had not made efforts to do so, then she would have made them. Nevertheless, she felt that he was carrying things a bit too far. He had been rude to her twice in the fortnight that they had been back on the unit, and on both occasions she had bitten back her replies, certain that his state of mind was a temporary one.

The changes that had taken place on the unit were more difficult for Claire to take. Sue had evidently attacked her role as relief sister with some gusto and had swept through the unit like a new broom, tidying, replacing and generally performing a premature spring clean. It was as if she had wanted to purge the unit of the memory of Alan Foster.

Claire found herself both delighted and bruised. It was a strange sensation which she put down to the fact, as sister, that she had never left the unit for as long as two weeks before.

As she went around the unit noting the changes and discovering how very efficient her staff nurse had been in control of it, Claire was reminded of her scan through the journals for a possible change of job.

At the first opportunity that presented itself Claire suggested to Sue that she might apply for a first-line management course. Sue looked up, surprised, from the drugs that she was checking at the medicine cupboard.

'That's very flattering,' she said, 'but I'm rather hoping not to have to give my life in the service of nursing,' she grinned at Claire.

'I know, Sue, but it would give you confidence. And, you never know, you might delay having a family and be glad of the extra cash one step up the ladder.'

'You make it sound tempting. But I think I'll stay here as a staff nurse if you'll have me for a bit longer.'

'Sue. I don't have to tell you how much we need you here. In fact, that's just what I'm thinking about.' Claire caught Sue's alarmed look.

'You're not thinking of leaving?' she burst out.

'No. Not at the moment,' Claire quietly replied. 'But I'd very much like to know you had a management course under your belt.'

'Okay, Claire, but only for you. Administration sends cold shivers down my spine . . .'

'Oh, does it Staff Nurse?'

Claire and Sue wheeled round simultaneously to find Humph standing glaring at them from the other side of the station. She had performed the impossible, for her, and crept up on them unheard. The Nursing Officer was in a laconic mood.

'Two weeks' relieving Sister Brown is enough to convince you that you are not cut out for administration, eh? And you seemed to be doing so nicely,' she enunciated crisply, every word laden. This was the cue that Claire needed.

'That was just what I was telling Staff Nurse, Miss Humphreys,' she said sweetly. 'I was suggesting to her that she might feel ready for a first-line management course.'

'And do you?' The administrative nurse glared at Sue, this time with an expression calculated to paralyse her speech.

'I do, actually, Miss Humphreys. I would like to go on

a course very much. Sister Brown is going to apply for me.' Sue's controlled response clearly took the Nursing Officer by surprise. Her face relaxed and she even smiled.

'I see Staff Nurse has emptied the unit for you, Sister.'

It was Claire's turn to pass the barbed tongue test. She smiled serenely.

'Would you like to take your round, Miss Humphreys? We were full last week, actually, but things have quietened down since. We have four patients today, all of them fairly well. I'll come round with you now.'

'Thank you, Sister. Everything seems very quiet. I expect it's the calm before the storm.' Miss Humphreys turned away and surveyed the unit with a critical eye.

Claire and Sue met each other's eyes briefly and Sue gave Claire the ghost of a wink.

'Oh, yes. I expect it is, Miss Humphreys,' Claire agreed placidly. 'That's how things go here, isn't it?'

She took the Nursing Officer round the unit, giving her a full rundown on each patient's condition. All were women and all of them in chronic renal failure and on their maintenance dialysis. The women had generated that unmistakable atmosphere that you find on any female ward; there was a calm, cosy, chatty feeling about the unit which was pleasant to work in and easy to miss when it was dispelled for some reason—usually the admission of a male patient. Claire liked the unit like this and so did the junior nursing staff, all of whom were quietly occupied with their patients.

Miss Humphreys left the unit less discreetly than she had entered it, casting a backward glance and a nod at Claire as she swung the doors open.

'I'll be expecting an application for a course for Staff, then Sister?' she pronounced over her shoulder.

'Yes, Miss Humphreys. I'll get that in to you as soon as possible,' Claire confirmed.

She popped her head around each of the cubicle doors as she made her way back down the unit to the nurses' station. The patients were in a lighthearted mood and had been on best behaviour during the round she had just conducted with the Nursing Officer. She thanked each one and told them lunch would be served very soon. She felt happy with the unit and the world, in spite of her private worries.

Approaching the station Claire was pleased to see Tony Fraser there, sitting with his back to her, half on and half off the desk, in his characteristic pose, talking to Sue. She was shaking her head. Claire reflected that these were the first few peaceful moments that she had had to share with Tony on the unit since they got back from the Lakes. Maybe the relaxed atmosphere would be reflected in Tony's mood.

She had almost reached the desk when he turned round, saw her, and, with an inexplicably hard glance, wished her a good morning. He called her 'Sister' in the formal manner which she had got used to since their return from holiday.

'Hello,' Claire greeted him cheerily in return, 'how's things with you?'

'Fine. Just off, actually.' The registrar pushed himself off the edge of the desk and smiled at Sue. 'See you then,' he said to her and then made off past Claire without another look in her direction.

Claire tried to hide her feelings, but she need not have bothered. Sue knew that she and Tony had been on holiday together, and although the staff nurse respected Claire enough not to make indiscreet inquiries, little had escaped her notice since the sister and doctor had returned to the unit.

'That was rude of him,' Sue now commented, too annoyed on her colleague's behalf to ignore the episode.

'Oh, it doesn't matter. I'm getting used to it,' Claire

sighed and shrugged her shoulders, following the retreating registrar with her eyes as she did so. 'What were
you talking about anyway?'

'Oh, he was just asking me if we were going to the
cheese and wine party in the residency tomorrow night
. . .' Sue stopped short, mid-sentence, as if she realised
the effect of her remark.

Claire felt it hit her. Tomorrow night . . . she had
completely forgotten the party, although Tony had mentioned it specifically while they were away, in connection
with their continuing to go out with one another after
they got back to work. Yet he had not mentioned it to
her again.

'Are you going?' she managed to ask Sue in a casual
voice.

The staff nurse looked at her gently.

'Oh, I don't think so, no,' she told her senior lightly.
'They're a real bore, these hospital parties, don't you
think?'

'They are, really,' Claire replied. 'Shall we give the
afternoon staff the report, then go for lunch together?'

'Good idea,' Sue said, smiling.

Claire spent Saturday on an early duty, trying not to
think too much about the wine and cheese party to which
she had not been invited. It was not that she wanted to go
to a party in the residency—Sue was right, they were
boring—but the fact that Tony had completely ignored
her, in spite of their previous agreement, that hurt her.

She had been so sure that he was wrong for her, so
certain that she did not want anything other than a
platonic relationship with him. Yet she remembered the
end of their holiday together with special pleasure. She
had begun to think that maybe he genuinely was interested in her and that perhaps the cold ambition which
she had always associated with him was, in fact, super-

ficial after all. She had to admit to herself that she was disappointed that he had been so offhand towards her since their return.

Fiona was away for her weekend off and the flat was empty and cold when she got home at five o'clock. Claire lit the gas fire in the sitting-room and thought vaguely about what she would eat that evening. She knew that Fiona had gone to spend the weekend with a girl she had trained with who was now living and working in West London. She pictured Fiona enjoying the last of the shopping in Oxford Street at this moment, immersed in the richness of the pre-Christmas displays. It would be lovely up there. Maybe she was planning on the cinema or a show tonight. Her friend would probably have planned a double date for them and Fiona would love that.

Fiona had not mentioned David Duncan again, Claire reflected. She was obviously stung by his reluctance to fall under her spell, in spite of what Tony had said in the Lakes. It was plain that Dr Duncan was actually not interested in Fiona, although Claire was a million miles from believing for one instant that Fiona was right in thinking that he was interested in her. For a shocked moment Claire stood still, beside the kitchen table, and fought back the tears that threatened to pour down her cheeks. It was a mistake to remember David Duncan. It was a mistake to think about Tony Fraser, or even of her reservations about him.

She took down a tin of mushroom soup from the cupboard and began automatically to pour it into a pan and heat it up. She would feel better when she'd eaten.

She sat down at the table and slowly sipped her soup, feeling the emptiness of the flat around her. She decided that she would run a hot bath for herself and have a long, deep soak, then get out and curl up in her favourite chair and escape into her book. She could go to bed later, she was not on duty until one o'clock tomorrow.

She had just turned the bath water on when the door bell went. She could not think who could be calling on her at this time on a Saturday evening and for one mad moment the thought went through her head that it might be Tony, sorry that he had forgotten to ask her before, wanting her to dress quickly and come to the residency party with him.

She ran down the stairs and opened the outside door, so pleased to have her lonely evening dispelled that she was already smiling as it swung back to reveal the solid form of David Duncan.

Claire gasped, then pulled herself together.

'Oh, Fiona isn't here,' she told him as calmly as she could, glad of the gloomy evening light of the street. 'She's got the weekend off. She's gone up to London to a friend's place.'

'I've not come to see Fiona,' he stated quietly. 'I've come to see you.' His face was shadowed and she could not make out the expression on it, but the words burned into her brain and made her dizzy.

'You'd better come in. It's cold out there,' she said.

Dr Duncan followed her up the steep stairs and into the flat. Claire showed him into the sitting-room and hurriedly excused herself to go and turn the bath water off. It was a merciful excuse. She looked at herself in the mirror over the basin and saw her own wild eyes staring back at her. What could he want with her? What would she say to him? She took a deep breath and tried to be calm. It was no use trying to tidy herself up. She would just have to cope as she was and hold her usual post-mortem afterwards.

'Would you like a cup of coffee or tea?' she managed to ask politely.

'Neither. Thank you.' He was still standing in the middle of the tiny sitting-room and Claire had to look up at him to ask her question. He looked down at her with clouded grey eyes.

'Do sit down,' she said again, formally.

'Thank you, I will.' He sat down on her favourite chair as if he belonged there. It was where he had sat the last time he had been here.

'I did not mean to be rude to you. On the Unit,' he said. Claire sat down on the settee opposite him, weakly. She waited for him to go on. 'But I was surprised to find you still at St Helen's,' he continued.

Claire found her voice. 'The surprise was not a pleasant one.'

Dr Duncan merely regarded her without flickering. His face seemed devoid of expression and older, so much older than she remembered it. In the soft sitting-room light, Claire could see the hard line of his chin, the set of his mouth and the hollow cheeks, so different from the youthful features that she had treasured in her memories of him.

'I did not mean you to form that impression,' he said, leaning back in the chair and staring hard at her. Claire took the look for as long as she could and then interrupted it with a rush of words which poured out unrehearsed, in spite of herself.

'I didn't know where you'd gone. When I came back you were gone and there was nobody whom I could ask. And I was upset and distracted at the time. Why didn't you contact me? You knew where I was. You just disappeared . . .' She broke off as the expression on his face changed.

'Does it matter where I went? Don't ask questions. It is of no concern to you; it wasn't then and it isn't now. I am here now. Isn't that all that matters?'

Claire felt herself go hot and then cold. It was as if she were dreaming. But this man was not the one of her dreams. He was the same man but devoid of the charac-

teristics that she had cherished. It was like a cruel
nightmare from which she could not wake up. And as if
she was dreaming she felt herself compelled to go on
with the scene, in spite of the fact that she wanted it to be
over.

'David . . .' she heard herself saying, 'please,
David . . .'

'Don't speak to me like that.' His voice was low. She
could hardly hear him.

'But I don't understand . . .' Claire began.

The doctor stood directly in front of her chair and
pulled her to her feet so that she was facing him, very
close.

'I don't want you to understand, Claire. Do you
understand that much? That is enough. I just want you,
not your understanding.'

Claire could feel the iron grip of his hands on her
shoulders. She tried to pull away, but it was to no avail.
He pulled her so that she could feel his hard chest against
her resistant breast and then he covered her face with
ruthless kisses. She waited with dread for his unfeeling
mouth to find hers, but he did not attempt to kiss her
there. He was holding her as if he wanted to squeeze the
breath out of her, but she felt breathless enough without
his hold. It was enough to realise in whose arms she was.

While all her finer feelings fought him, her baser ones
accepted his embrace, his passion and his kisses, and she
was powerless to resist. He let her go quite suddenly, as
if he had lost the physical energy to hold her, and Claire
fell back into the settee. He sat down wearily in the seat
he had occupied before. He regarded her as if what had
just happened had never taken place and he had never
moved out of the chair.

'How about that cup of tea or coffee?' he asked
flippantly.

'First I want to know why you are doing this,' Claire

was surprised by her own anger. Fury spread up through her as her blood had seemed to spread through her during his kisses, and her head felt as if it were full of molten lead. 'I want to know why you are behaving like this towards me. Why are you here? How dare you sit there waiting for coffee as if nothing has happened between us?'

'Nothing has happened between us,' he responded in a flat voice. 'Yet.'

'But,' Claire began, almost unable to believe her own ears, 'you are amazing. I should throw you out. You walk in here, having ignored the fact that we knew one another years ago, and . . .'

'And, nothing . . .' He had got to his feet again and was leaning on the mantelpiece beside the fire. The soft glow from the fire softened his face and gave it back some of its long-ago handsomeness. Claire felt herself melting.

'David. I am pleased to see you. It's just that . . . you seem so . . .'

Claire bent her head in embarrassment and misery and covered her face with her hands. She was determined not to cry, but it was hard not to do so. She lifted her head again and carefully picked up her coffee. He was looking at her from his position beside the fire.

'Listen, Claire. I want to see you from time to time. Will you come out with me next weekend?' He spoke patiently, as if to a child.

'Yes,' said Claire simply, 'I'll do that.'

'I've got to go now. It's late,' he glanced at his watch and Claire realised that he had been there for nearly two hours—the longest two hours of her life.

'Yes,' she said again, 'I suppose it is.'

He crossed the room and Claire got automatically to her feet. Before she knew what was happening she was back in his arms and this time he went straight to her

mouth, searching for her, bruising her with the violence
of his kiss. It was a travesty of all she had ever hoped for
from a kiss, especially a kiss from this man. But she
yielded to him and felt the blood rise and drain from her
limbs and body and a burning longing for it never to
end.

At last he let her go and she stood, looking up at him,
half dazed with the longing he left in her.

'I think,' she began shakily, 'I think you have the
wrong idea about me. You cannot play with me . . .'

'I do not have the wrong idea about you. I do not want
to play with you. It is you who have the wrong ideas,' he
stated calmly.

Claire took a deep breath. 'I see,' she said.

'I doubt that,' he answered her, quickly.

'I think,' she began again, 'that Fiona might make you
happier than I can. She is quite upset by your ill attention
to her.'

'Oh, is she now? That would leave you nicely free to
continue your liaison with Tony Fraser, wouldn't it?'

Claire held her breath at this, but she did not have to
wait long for him to go on.

'But, unfortunately for you, I am not in the least
interested in Miss Shore.'

'And I am not interested in Dr Fraser. Apart from
professionally, of course . . .'

'I'm aware of that. I should not be here tonight if I was
not,' Dr Duncan told her.

So that was why Tony was behaving the way he had
been behaving towards her. Claire was stunned. She did
not have time to put all the pieces together mentally
before Dr Duncan was gone. He did not attempt to
touch her again. He simply opened the door at the top of
the stairs for himself and went down to the street.

Claire decided not to tell Fiona about Dr Duncan's visit

to the flat. It seemed to her that she would be rubbing salt into the wound that she knew her friend had had inflicted by the surgical registrar.

She listened to Fiona's very occasional comments about Dr Duncan's behaviour in theatre without commenting on them, and hoped that Fiona did not notice any difference in her attitude now from earlier. If she did, she certainly didn't show it.

The Saturday that Claire had promised to go out with Dr Duncan was very cold. Claire walked through the park to the shopping centre as usual on her day off. She remembered walking over the crisp, frosted grass that day of her dental appointment. It seemed an age ago. How she would have longed then to be in the position she was today, with the prospect of a whole evening with David Duncan ahead of her. Yet she felt unnerved. She had been shocked at her own response to him. She seemed to be incapable of rejecting his passionate advances.

Fiona was on a late duty, thank goodness, Claire thought. She could not have lied about where she was going. In the end she put on a clean pair of black cord trousers with a black polo-necked sweater. As she was combing her hair she smiled ruefully at herself in the mirror. All in black. You're not going to a funeral, you know, she told herself. Yes, you are, replied her inner self, you're going to your own.

She thanked him as he helped her into his car. The car puzzled her too. It was flashy, smart, not the sort of thing that fitted in with his personality as she had known it. *As she had known it.* She could not get used to this new David Duncan at all.

He told her that they were going for a drive.

'Ah,' was all she could think of to say to this. It was dark: a cold, dark, late autumn evening.

'How are you?' he enquired brusquely.

'Fine. Really fine,' Claire said, and then, to fill the silence that fell between them, 'the unit's busy again though.'

'For God's sake let's not talk shop,' Dr Duncan snapped back at her and Claire stared out of the dark window next to her, trying to hide her unhappiness.

'Talk about yourself,' he demanded.

'There's nothing much to tell,' Claire said. 'I left the medical ward after . . . after . . .' she took a deep breath. This was stupid. Why shouldn't she tell him? She at least would try to behave reasonably in this relationship. She began again, 'My parents died. In an accident. I went to work on the Renal Unit and got the Sister's post there. I've been there ever since.'

'Not very adventurous of you.'

Claire broke at this. She turned to him in the darkened car.

'Would you mind taking me home?' she asked. 'I don't want to stay any longer in your company. You seem only to want to be rude to me and to hurt me, and I can do without both.' She was surprised at her own voice, hot with anger as it was.

Dr Duncan slowed the car and she thought he was going to turn round and head back towards Elchester, but instead he drew in to a lay-by. He stopped the car and put the hand brake on, then sat silently, looking out of the windscreen at the oncoming car headlights. Claire caught his expression in the sweeping beams as they passed. He looked sad and trapped. But their past and her secret knowledge of his illness was an unspoken bond between them.

At last she felt his arm around the back of her seat and she was gathered towards him. She accepted his hard kiss, although it hurt her, and then she pulled away from him.

'David. This is childish. Only children kiss in parked

cars. Why don't we go somewhere. To eat. Or for a drink. Why are you doing this to us?'

'I don't want to talk to you,' his voice came to her, strangled, as if he was forcing the words out between unparted lips.

'And I don't want . . . this . . . from you,' she heard her own voice say, although she was longing for him to draw her back to him, to take her to him again. As if he read her innermost thoughts, Dr Duncan moved towards her in the darkness and kissed her again, this time less forcefully, but for long enough for her to feel his hot breath on her face.

Released, Claire sat back in the passenger seat while he started the car and began to drive back to Elchester. He was driving fast, too fast, but Claire was too numb to feel any fear. She had no idea what he would do next, but, dimly, she wished he would take her back to the flat and that he would then leave her to her thoughts.

She sat unmoving, waiting for the car to stop. When it did so, she did not recognise the street in which they had parked. She got out of the car and together they walked, he leading her. On the corner of the street they came to a noisy wine bar. Claire had never been to it, but she now recalled having heard the student nurses talking about the place, which had opened fairly recently.

'Sit down,' he ordered when they came to a table with two seats at it. Claire obeyed. She could hardly hear herself think.

She waited until he returned from the bar with a bottle of chilled white wine and two glasses. Claire was hungry, or she would have been if she had been a little calmer. The last thing that she wanted to do was to drink on her empty stomach. She took a sip of the bright, astringent wine. At least it took away the smell of tobacco which had found its way into her mouth.

'Is that good?' he asked her.

'Fine,' she shouted, 'but I can't hear myself think in here. Why did we come here?'

'Because we can't hear ourselves think. That's why.'

Miserably, Claire allowed him to pour her another glass of wine, and she tried to concentrate on the guitar and the song the player was singing. It was, she realised, an old number called 'A Simple Twist of Fate'. Apt, she thought, with uncharacteristic bitterness. She felt as if she could have done without this twist of fate. Her dream had been so much happier than this reality. What was he trying to do to her?

They sat in the wine bar for an hour, neither of them speaking. Sometimes Claire caught Dr Duncan's expression as he glanced at her, and she tried to read it but could not do so. She grew angrier and angrier. The noise and music had the desired effect from his point of view. He had her company without conversation.

'I don't know whether you have any more plans for this evening,' she said eventually, 'but I'd like you to take me home. If you don't mind.'

They drove silently back to the flat. Claire felt exhausted by the last few hours. The car came to a standstill outside the flat and David turned the headlights off.

'You don't like me much, do you?' he asked in a level voice. He was sitting as he had done at first in the lay-by, staring out of the darkened windscreen. But here, in the quiet of Monmouth Gardens, there were no sweeping headlights of oncoming cars by whose light Claire could read his features.

'It's not true . . .' she whispered, 'it's not true that I don't like you . . .' She could not go on.

'When is your next evening off?' he asked her in a more normal voice.

She had told him and agreed to see him again before she'd had time to think. She tried to open her door and had to look for the right catch but he did not attempt to help her to find it, or to turn the lights on ready to drive away either.

'Until Wednesday then,' Claire murmured, and got out of the car. He said goodbye and continued to sit there while Claire fought the wish that he would get out and make some tender move towards her.

She opened the front door, glancing upwards to the lighted sitting-room window above as she did so. Thank goodness, Fiona was in. She could not have borne to have got home to an empty flat this evening. It was not until she had reached the top of the stairs and put her key into the lock that she heard the car rev up and leave. She breathed a sigh of relief.

Fiona heard the door and shouted 'hello' through to the hall from her seat in the sitting-room. Claire did not stop to take her coat off, but went straight in, dropped it on to the settee and sat down on top of it.

'Where've you been?' Fiona said, looking up mischievously. But one glance at her friend's face changed her look to one of concern.

'Oh, out,' Claire said simply.

'Come on, Claire. You look awful. Where have you been?'

'Don't, Fiona. I'll be all right. Honestly,' Claire told her flatmate, 'I'm just tired and hungry, that's all.'

She went into the kitchen and made herself an omelette and a mug of coffee and another cup of coffee for Fiona, then picked up a knife and fork and carried her meal back into the other room.

'Thanks,' Fiona said, taking her coffee and balancing it on the arm of the chair in which she was sitting, filing her nails.

Claire finished her omelette and took the plate back through to the kitchen. She felt much better for having eaten it. The hot coffee slid down and comforted her, warming and cheering her from the inside.

When she looked up from her cup she saw that Fiona was sitting with hers held in both hands, looking at her over it. Suddenly, Claire could not contain herself any longer.

'Fiona, I shall have to tell you,' she said, 'I've been out with David Duncan this evening.'

The impact this information had upon her flatmate was obvious from the look on her face.

'With *whom*?' she asked in open amazement.

'I know, I didn't want to tell you in case it upset you. I knew you liked him.'

'But . . . how . . . ?' Fiona stammered.

'He came round here,' Claire admitted, 'I thought at first he'd come to see you and ask you out . . . but it was me . . .'

Fiona laughed.

'Well that's a turn-up for the books,' she said. 'It must be history being made. I bet that surprised you; with your self confidence I bet you asked him if he was absolutely sure it was you he wanted,' she giggled at her friend.

'You're not too upset?' Claire ventured.

''Course I'm not. I'm pleased. Really I am.'

Claire smiled at Fiona and felt more relaxed. She had not realised up until now how guilty she had been feeling about this aspect of her new relationship with David Duncan.

'What's he like then? I told you it was you he was interested in. Did he take you to that awful dingy pub he took me to, or was it a candlelit dinner for you?'

'Oh, I wish it had been,' Claire said and lapsed into thoughtfulness.

'What do you mean?' Fiona asked.

'I used to know him before . . .' Claire began.

'Before when?'

Claire felt the tears that she had held back for so long

that evening hot, pricking behind her lids, and this time she did not resist them. She felt overwhelmingly relieved at being able to tell someone about her feelings.

Fiona got up quickly and came over to where her flatmate was sitting and put a protective arm about her shoulders. It was a total reversal of their usual roles, and Claire smiled through her tears at the thought.

'It is a turn up for the books, isn't it? You having to play agony aunt to me for a change.'

Claire took the tissue that Fiona offered her and dried her eyes. Fiona sat down softly beside her.

'Tell me about it, Claire,' she said.

Claire began and told her the whole story—or most of it—right up until their meeting again in the dentist's surgery.

'I thought he behaved strangely towards you when I brought him in for coffee that night after the emergency,' Fiona said, 'and now it all falls into place. But why is he being such a pig to you? I can't understand that bit at all.'

'Tony told me that he'd been ill,' Claire said, her heart tight as the words formed, 'I think that might have something to do with it.'

She turned to face her friend. She still could not bring herself to give David's illness its name out loud.

'But it's so awful, Fiona. It makes me so unhappy. I've never felt like this before and I just can't seem to control my feelings while I'm with him. I do things that I've never done before and feel things that I never thought I'd ever feel. And even when I know that I should stop and think and make him stop and think, I can't seem to do it . . . I just never want to stop . . .' she tailed off and stopped talking, holding her breath while she thought of David Duncan's mouth on hers . . .

'It's because you've never been in love before, Claire. That's all,' Fiona told her quietly.

'But I'm not in love,' Claire burst out, 'I can't be. He's too horrible. This is just a physical thing. That's what I hate about it. It makes me hate myself.'

'All right. So you're not in love with him. But you mustn't feel so guilty all the time, Claire. Give it time. See how things go.'

This calm advice settled over Claire like a soft cloud.

'Meantime, I think I'll make us both another cup of coffee before we get some sleep. Or would you prefer hot chocolate?'

'No. Coffee would be lovely. Thank you, Fiona. I don't know what I'd have done without you.'

'Then you know how I usually feel about you,' Fiona said from the kitchen.

'It was awful,' Claire found herself laughing rather light-headedly between her words, 'he took me to this awful wine bar where we couldn't talk because of the noise. It was full of the most peculiar people and he bought us this wine that neither of us wanted, just so that he didn't have to talk to me, and he 'phoned up St Helen's to see when you'd be off-duty,' Claire said.

'Good grief. You have had a nice evening. He 'phoned to make sure I'd be out when you got back and I wasn't, eh? Charming, I'm sure.'

Claire woke up refreshed the next morning. She and Fiona walked to the hospital together, muffled up against the biting November winds, the only people in the park.

'I feel a lot better for having told you,' Claire confessed.

'Funnily enough, I feel a lot better for you having told me,' Fiona replied. 'I can be as unpleasant as he deserves now. Before, he was getting away with murder in theatre. All because I entertained secret hopes that he would turn out to be the most devastating lover I'd ever had. Well, he's had it now, so to speak.'

Claire laughed out loud. 'You're wicked, Fiona.'

'But I tell you what,' Fiona went on, 'I think your Dr Duncan is going to be less than popular with his chief if he carries on giving him no notice of illness the way he tends to. It's just not good enough going off sick at the drop of a hat without telling anybody until it's too late to get a locum. I'd be furious if one of my nurses did it. Wouldn't you?'

'Yes. I would,' Claire answered Fiona. She could not tell her how suddenly he could be incapacitated by his kidney disease.

'He's Matthewson's blue-eyed boy at the moment. But I don't know how long the old man can go on making excuses for him.'

'I'm surprised he went into surgery,' Claire mused out loud, in a desperate bid to change the subject.

'Oh, why?' Fiona asked.

'Because he was all against modern heroics and all for traditional medicine,' Claire went on. 'He was super with the patients. A real bedside doctor.'

'Was he indeed?' Fiona rejoined.

'Yes. He was,' Claire could not keep the regret out of her voice.

'He seems to have changed quite a bit since his youth,' Fiona remarked. 'I'm quite glad you're not in my shoes. You'd be thoroughly disenchanted if you had to work with him, I assure you.'

'Yes,' Claire said, 'I believe I would.'

They had reached the hospital and passed through the ornate gates into the ample grounds that surrounded it. Fiona breathed a deep breath of air.

'My last for eight hours,' she explained to Claire with a grin.

'You make it sound awful,' Claire said, 'Anybody

would think you hated your job sometimes.'

'Oh, I do,' Fiona replied, 'Just filling in time until the right man comes along, you know.' She smiled stoically at this gross self-misrepresentation.

'You're not a very good liar,' Claire told her.

'See you later,' Fiona returned, 'I'll come and meet you off the unit at four thirty. Will you be ready by then?'

'Should be,' Claire reassured her. 'Wait in my sitting-room in the corridor if I'm still busy. I shouldn't be long after that. The unit isn't that busy.'

She felt lighter hearted than she had for some time as she made her way to the unit. She felt lucky to have Fiona as a flatmate, and she was still amused by the role reversal that had occurred last night.

She had barely finished taking the report from the night nurses when Miss Humphreys sailed in through the unit doors and the junior nurses scattered at the sight of her, dispatching themselves to their work in record time.

'Got the dates through for that Staff Nurse of yours,' Miss Humphreys announced as she approached Claire's station desk.

'Thank you, Miss Humphreys,' she responded politely, 'When is she going?'

'Directly after Christmas. First week after New Year. Now I hope this doesn't mean we're losing you, Sister Brown?'

Her directness caught Claire momentarily unawares.

'Oh, no. At least, I don't think so. No, Miss Humphreys,' she stammered.

'Good thing too,' the Nursing Officer said, 'All these young things getting married and having babies. I expect Staff Nurse will hardly be back before she's off having one herself. It's a waste of funds, so it is. You'll tell her then,' the Nursing Officer stated uncompromisingly.

'Yes. Of course I will. Thank you, Miss Humphreys.'

'You look better for your holiday, Sister,' the older woman said.

'But I've been back a month,' Claire said, smiling.

'Quite so,' Miss Humphreys said, 'I'll be back for a round later.'

Claire saw her out of the unit, closing the doors gently behind the large woman. Miss Humphreys was someone to be reckoned with, but she was a welcome arm of the administrative system, closer to the unit than matron had ever been in previous times, and more approachable than her manner suggested—as Claire knew from personal experience. There was little that Humph missed and nobody more sympathetic to a genuine request for assistance than she.

'Sue,' she said when the Staff Nurse appeared for her late duty, 'your management course dates have come through. I'm afraid they're directly after Christmas.'

Sue came up to the station and looked at the sheet of paper that Claire held out to her.

'That's okay,' she said, 'I don't mind at all. What are we going to do about Christmas anyway? We were going to discuss it.'

'Yes,' Claire responded. 'You take Christmas off and I'll take some time later.'

'But . . . you always seem to work over Christmas,' Sue said, 'I don't mind for once.'

'No. It's your first Christmas together. You take it. I've only just come back from holiday,' Claire insisted.

'But so have I,' Sue said, then, seeing the look that Claire gave her she relented. 'You've made up your mind, haven't you?'

'Yes. I have.'

'Thank you, Claire. I'll enjoy it, and I just hope we're not too busy for you to enjoy it too.'

With this important decision settled, Claire felt happier about Sue's badly timed management course, and they spent the rest of the day planning what improvements they would make in the structure of the patients' day in the New Year. Miss Humphreys had left some reports on the subject with Claire the week before and this was the first time that they had had to talk about them since they'd both read and digested them.

Claire did not notice the time passing, and it was with surprise that she glanced up at the clock above the station and found it said a quarter to five. Fiona would be waiting for her. She had not noticed her coming into the unit, but she was probably in her room in the corridor.

Claire said a hurried goodbye to Sue and made her way down the unit towards her sitting-room. It wasn't until she had drawn level with the door that she heard low voices. At first she thought they came out of the doctors' room opposite her own, but then she realised that they came from hers. She could hear Tony's voice, unmistakably, from inside. Sometimes he used her room to talk to relatives in private when the doctors' room was occupied, so Claire knocked softly on the door and waited to be asked in.

After a moment the door opened and Tony brushed past her as he came out, mumbling something which could have been an apology. To her amazement, Claire saw that Fiona was inside the room looking somewhat less than composed.

'Oh, Claire, it's you,' Fiona said unnecessarily.

'Well, yes. Of course it is. What's the matter, Fiona?'

'Nothing,' said her flatmate, unconvincingly.

Claire closed the door behind her and stood looking at her friend, standing, rather flushed, in the middle of the square of carpet that covered the centre of the floor.

'It's Dr Fraser. He's just asked me out,' Fiona almost gasped.

Claire could not help laughing at the expression on her friend's face.

'And did you accept?' she asked.

'Yes,' said Fiona, pushing her hair back with both hands as if she'd just been through a whirlwind, 'I did.'

'Well, that's all right then,' Claire said, 'I hope it improves his temper.'

She picked up her coat. 'I feel exhausted,' she said.

As they left the hospital together Claire thought how she envied her friend her carefree attitude towards life and love.

It seemed like minutes rather than days until her next date with David Duncan, and Claire got more and more nervous, and even played with the idea of ringing him in theatre to cancel their arrangement. Only the thought that Fiona might answer the telephone in person, or be next to the 'phone while she spoke to him, put her off the idea.

Fiona was at least sensitive enough not to ask her what she was going to wear, or where they were going, but this might have been partly, or even wholly because she had a date with Tony Fraser the same evening. She did not attempt to disguise her enthusiasm for her own date and had pumped Claire endlessly since he'd asked her out, for information about him and details about the holiday in the Lakes—about which Claire had all but forgotten.

'He's quite good-looking, isn't he? Don't you think so?' Fiona asked Claire for the third time, as they got home to the flat that evening.

'Yes,' Claire replied, 'he is. Lots of people think so, anyway.'

'What was that you said about him being inaccessible?'

'Oh. That's what all the new nurses on the unit seem to think. I'm surprised you haven't seen him before. You're on the hospital social scene enough. But I suppose you don't bother with all those residency things he used to take me to,' Claire remarked, smiling.

'Dreadful. No, thank goodness!'

'He's been saving his candlelit supper for you,' Claire joked back at her friend. But Fiona just gave her a rueful look and remembered the last time they'd talked like this.

Claire was quite glad that Fiona had arranged to meet Tony half an hour earlier than she and David were meeting. She wanted the peace and quiet to dress and think before she met him in the Italian restaurant in Elchester. She had purposely arranged to meet him there, so that she could walk there and not be waiting nervously in the flat for him to come for her.

She dressed in a soft beige wool dress and belted it at the waist. It was her favourite dress, comfortable and well fitting. She knew it suited her and that made her feel more confident than usual. She draped a toning coloured silk scarf around her shoulders and tied it loosely at the front. The muted browns and oranges looked good on her.

Walking to the town in the early evening light, Claire decided that she would remain composed and dignified that night. At least if they were going to have a meal there would be a prescribed pattern to their evening. Claire dreaded what had happened last time they'd met happening a second time.

She had begun to wonder what she had worried about by the time their coffee came. David had been distant but fairly pleasant company, in spite of his prickliness whenever Claire broached a subject which meant him imparting personal information. So she was caught off-guard when he suddenly said, 'So your flatmate and Tony have a date tonight too?'

Claire affirmed this fact.

'And how do you feel about that, Claire?' Dr Duncan asked, staring hard at her. His voice was bitter.

'What do you mean, how do I feel? I'm very pleased for them. Aren't you?' Claire replied.

He shrugged and sat back in his chair.

'I'd have thought you might feel rather sore about it,' he continued, 'after your holiday together. You must have got quite close.'

'I don't like the tone of that remark,' Claire said, as calmly as she could.

'Nevertheless, I should think it's difficult to take, your flatmate muscling in like that,' Dr Duncan persisted in a hard voice.

'David, it isn't like that at all. What are you talking about?' Claire felt her anger rising.

'Of course. Tony and you are just good friends. But not, if I know Tony, because he invented the rules of the game. You like to have things on your own terms, don't you?'

Claire fought the tide of confusion that flooded through her. She could not imagine why he was treating her like this, but she was not going to sit there and take it from him. She stood up and left the table and, collecting her coat beside the door, walked out of the restaurant. Dr Duncan did not appear to follow her, or even to look round as she left the place. Outside Claire stood for a moment to let her heart settle. Then she began to walk briskly homewards. She had nearly reached the park when she heard the car draw up beside her.

'Get in, Claire. Please,' he asked her, his voice soft, the way she had so often remembered it. The Scottish lilt was only recognisable when he spoke like this. When he hardened his voice it seemed to disappear, as if his tone did not deserve the music of his native dialect.

'No. Thank you,' Claire said, and continued to walk on. The car came up beside her again.

'Please,' he pleaded, 'I'd like to apologise to you.'

In spite of herself, Claire found herself walking round and getting into the front of the car beside him. He drove silently towards Monmouth Gardens and when they were at the end of the street, Claire could see that there was nobody back at the flat yet. She wondered whether or not she should ask him in and decided against it.

'Thank you for the meal and for the lift,' Claire said, and undid her door. He got out and came up to the front door of the flat with her. He put his hand on the door so that she could not open it.

'You're not going to ask me in?' he asked.

'No,' she responded flatly, 'I'm not.'

'Listen, Claire . . .'

'I don't want to listen. You listen to me—I am not, and never was, in love with Tony Fraser . . .'

Claire could see the dim outline of David Duncan's face in the light of the street lamp. His eyes were troubled, yet as hard as ice. She still could not look at him without remembering . . .

'Good,' he said, his lips hardly moving. Then she felt herself drawn towards him and he held her against him for what seemed like a year before finding her lips and forcing them apart with his.

Her heart seemed to beat in her throat and she could hardly breathe. She felt as if she was melting, as if the only solid part of her was his strong encircling arms. His passion seemed all the more powerful for its silence. He did not say her name, he made no avowals, he paid her no compliments, and yet their bodies understood one another and the strength of her own responses left Claire weak.

When she opened her eyes he was looking down into her face, his own eyes unreadable, dark, grey. He straightened and let her go.

Claire blindly found her keys and opened the door.

He left her there and walked to his car, unlocked it and got inside. Claire ran up the stairs to the flat and got inside the comforting familiarity of the cosy sitting-room as quickly as she could. Before she had had time to switch the light on she heard the sound of David's car departing.

It was two hours later, after midnight, when she woke out of her troubled half-sleep to hear the whispering voices of Fiona and Tony, interspersed with muted laughter, in the hall.

Their relaxation was in such sharp contrast to the atmosphere of the evening she had just experienced, that it hurt. Claire realised that she could not go on like this with David Duncan. She had to come to terms with the fact that he was no longer the man she had admired and cared for so deeply, and she must put an end to their affair. She did not want a relationship like this, especially not with him, of all people. It was as far removed from her dreams as it could possibly be.

CHAPTER FIVE

Two weeks later Claire was walking home from St Helen's. It was the week before Christmas. There were only another two working days until her days off, and then it would be Christmas Eve and Sue would be off on her holiday and Claire would have yet another working Christmas on the unit.

The thought of Sue and her new husband celebrating the festive season together for the first time left her with an inner ache of unfulfilment. She tried to banish it, feeling ashamed at her hidden envy of her staff nurse.

And she still hadn't managed to bring her relationship with Dr Duncan to a satisfactory close. She felt ashamed of this too. She had made sure she was out when she thought he might telephone and then had failed to ring him back in response to his several messages to her.

She dreaded seeing him. The memory of that last meeting still hurt her, and yet she seemed to be incapable of doing anything final about their affair. Each time she felt hardened into resolve and was about to pick up the telephone, she was stopped by the cherished memory of a rare tender look from him.

She reached the door of the flat, still anguishing over her problem, and had almost decided to excuse herself until after Christmas. After all, she needed all her attention for the unit for the next week or so. She would spend her days off before Christmas shopping and posting things to her aunts, buying a few things for herself and stocking up the flat with things to eat over Christmas. She might even buy a tree; Fiona would be back to enjoy it with her on Boxing Day.

The telephone was ringing in the flat—Claire could hear it the moment she opened the door on to the street. She raced up the stairs, her heart in her mouth. She could not find the upstairs key in her rush, and fumbled for it, cursing under her breath. Fiona was still on duty and there was nobody in. At last she burst into the hall and slammed the door behind her. She rushed into the sitting-room and picked up the telephone just as the ringing died.

'Hello . . . hello . . .' she said breathlessly. But the dial tone was all she heard. It had probably just been Fiona, wanting to know if there was anything she should buy for supper on her way home. The shops would be closed in half an hour.

Claire went and put the kettle on for tea. She would be glad when Fiona got home—she hoped that she did not have a date with Tony tonight. It would be so nice to have company to watch the television, eat and talk with. She didn't seem to see much of Fiona since the start of her romance with Tony Fraser. They seemed completely involved with one another.

The shrill tones of the telephone broke in upon Claire's thoughts and she put the mug she was holding down with a clatter upon the draining-board.

'Yes?' she said into the 'phone.

'Why have you been avoiding me, Claire, why?'

It was David Duncan.

'I . . . I . . .' Claire began.

'I want to see you, Claire.'

He sounded desperate, angry but controlled. His voice was low, hardly audible.

'All right,' Claire heard herself agreeing in a whisper.

'When are you off duty?'

'The two days before Christmas Eve,' she responded.

'I'll come and pick you up on the first of those two evenings. At seven. You will be there? Claire?'

Claire swallowed hard.

'Yes,' she said, 'I will be here.'

'Until then,' he said, and hung up.

Claire experienced confusion, anticipation, relief and dread, and the conflicting emotions drained all the strength from her. She sat down beside the telephone table. She was still sitting there when Fiona whistled her way into the flat. She was producing a barely recognisable version of 'Hark the Herald Angels Sing', and it made Claire smile. She got up and was in the kitchen filling the teapot by the time Fiona had joined her there.

'Hello. Oh, it's nice to be home. What a day! Matthewson in a filthy mood all morning; filthier this afternoon. Talk about Christmas spirit . . . so much for that. Huh! Oh, great. A cuppa.'

But, in spite of her words, Fiona looked bright, cheerful and flatteringly fresh-faced from the bitter outside air.

'I'm really pleased to see you,' Claire said.

'Look what I've bought,' Fiona continued, her tea in one hand as she unpacked a carrier bag she'd brought in with her.

'I've got a pound of mandarines; two pounds of Cox's, walnuts, brazil nuts and even a pound of chocolates. The festive season has arrived at Monmouth Gardens if not at the General Theatre suite, St Helen's Hospital. I've got a passion for fruit at the moment . . .'

'Oh, I thought it was for Tony Fraser,' Claire grinned at her friend.

'Mmmm, him too,' she agreed cheerfully.

'Are you going out tonight?' Claire asked as casually as she could.

'No. He's on call and we're both too tired. We're going out tomorrow.'

'Oh, good. I was looking forward to a quiet evening at

home with my flatmate. She seems to be out half the time nowadays. I miss her.'

'And I miss you too, silly,' Fiona rejoined, 'but that's what happens when two people fall in love.'

'Which two people?' Claire asked, only half-jesting.

'Oops, sorry. Things going badly, Claire?'

Claire had not told her flatmate what had been going on—not that anything had—for the past few weeks.

'Not really. Never mind. Let's put the fruit out in the big earthenware dish next door. It'll look lovely in that.' She went to get the dish, not least to avoid the scrutiny of her friend who, with increasing ease lately, read her face with poignant accuracy.

'Shall we get a Christmas tree?' Claire called over her shoulder.

'Yes, let's. Poor old you, working Christmas Day,' said Fiona.

'Oh, I don't mind,' Claire said, and she suddenly found that she didn't and that her misgivings had disappeared.

She went on duty for her last early shift before her two days off preceding Christmas Eve with a light heart. She was seeing David tonight. The park shone in winter sunshine; silver, gold and bronze. Children played under the trees, boisterous with their school holidays and anticipation of Christmas to come. The sight of them further buoyed up Claire's spirit.

Christmas had approached slowly at St Helen's. The old hospital had begun its gentle, dignified preparations a week or so before, gradually allowing gay festivities to soften the stark corridors, the bare walls and the clinically white departments.

Bit by bit the wards had been transformed. During the quiet hours in the early afternoon, when the two day shifts of nurses overlapped, ward sisters had abandoned their teaching sessions in favour of ward decoration, and everybody with an iota of talent had been conscripted in to help. There was always more than a hint of competition between wards for the best decorations, and this was fiercest among the older sisters.

These older sisters were the barometer of the relaxation that occurred in the hospital as Christmas approached. And it did relax. A great tree was erected in the main hall to the sounds of muffled cursing and grunting on the part of the four porters who had been given the job. They would never have admitted how pleased they were to have it assigned to them, and they treated the task with apparent indifference but hidden excitement.

Student nurses from the school were traditionally responsible for decorating the tree, and they were given time off from their lectures to do so. They were also responsible for the huge bunches of mistletoe and holly which hung above the doors to the residency, staff dining-room and coffee rooms, the tiny internal Post Office, and the shop. But the shop itself, under the watchful eyes of the faithful ladies from the Women's Voluntary Service, was decorated with careful ebullience. It was festooned with red paper bells of massive proportions, tinsel, and large bunches of berryless plastic holly.

The sister in each ward decided where the tree went. In some of the older Nightingale wards its traditional place was in the centre, between the two long rows of beds that stretched from the nurses' station at the ward door to the sluices and bathrooms at the other end. Some of these wards had been 'upgraded' at St Helen's and a dayroom had been built on, along with new bathrooms and nurses' facilities at the far end, and in these wards Sister might choose to put the tree in the dayroom where all the ambulant patients could enjoy it.

But the favourite place remained the centre of the ward where it could be equally enjoyed by all.

The rather subdued festivities in the adult wards were amplified a hundredfold in the children's wards where, to squeals of delight and excitement, fairy playgrounds were being created by nurses and doctors whose hidden talents for painting and drawing had lain dormant since last year.

In one of the children's surgical wards Snow White and the Seven Dwarfs strode around the ward from one glass partition to another, their forest abode suggested by fir trees and sleighs and woodland scenes on every window. In another ward, Little Red Riding Hood and scenes from A Christmas Carol dominated the ward and in another, a huge Santa welcomed visitors at the door, while, within, between the cots, reindeer ran and bright sacks of presents seemed to spill from the windows on to the floor of the ward. Bright silver paper stars and moons hung on every cot and hung from every light, making each small bed look like a fairy cradle.

All the children who were well enough were always sent home for Christmas, and those that remained were a special focus of attention for nurses who worked over the Christmas period. The night staff on Christmas Eve would spend every quiet moment during the night packing up presents, those that came out of the ward fund and those little things they had bought themselves for each child, putting them into stockings with the traditional tangerine, nut and piece of coal, and hanging them on the end of each cot for the morning. A glass of sherry was taken during this important task and Night Sister would end up in a poor way if she did not refuse many a glass during her rounds on Christmas Eve.

Christmas morning would see many of the nurses who were officially off duty, coming in to visit 'their' children, bringing small gifts of their own. There was an air of unique excitement as the little patients unpacked their presents to the strains of carols from the red-caped group of nurses who stood under the tree on Christmas morning.

The memory of Christmasses as a young student nurse brought a lump to Claire's throat as she walked through the old hospital that morning and saw the preparations going on around her. She had always sung carols with the group that went round the wards and, as a student, she used often to be moved to tears at the sight of the patients who were separated from their loved ones at this time of year.

Christmas Eve: the carol singing. It was just three days off, and yet the time between then and now seemed to Claire to stretch for an eternity. Before she set off around the wards, secure in the traditional pattern of her working Christmasses, Claire had to face Dr David Duncan and her feelings for him. It could not be put off any longer and her evening with him tomorrow loomed large on her horizon.

Claire hung her coat behind the door of her sitting-room and breathed in the stuffy atmosphere of the centrally heated room. She crossed to the window, thinking she'd open it a little for an hour or so to freshen the air, and it was as she passed her desk that she caught sight of the envelope addressed to her in an unfamiliar hand.

She picked it up slowly, turning it over for clues as to its author, before opening it. A scrap of paper from a drug company's advertising jotting pad fell out of the envelope. She read:

'Forget tonight. Will be in touch. Apologies. David.'

Her eyes pricked at the crude abruptness of the message. She put the note back into the envelope and the envelope into the pocket of her jeans. Then she changed and went on duty with all the composure of a sentenced man.

So that was that. He had done the deed for her. He had wanted to break it off too and had lacked the courage up until now, just as she herself had done. In a curious, cowardly way, Claire was relieved.

In another corner of her soul she was desolate. Her dreams had come to nothing. She could never again trust her feelings, for if she had been so deeply certain of this man and he had proved so utterly unworthy of her feelings and had, far from returning them, rejected them completely, how could she ever dare to dream again?

Claire took the report and then delegated tasks, patients to nurses, and general responsibilities for the day, then she asked who could paint and who had the artistic qualities needed to turn the unit into a spectacle more appropriate to the season. The students allowed themselves childish grins of delight at the suggestion and Sue and the junior staff nurse took off in the direction of the hall cupboard where the decorations had been hidden since last year.

The atmosphere of the unit took on that of a carnival. All the three patients who had dialysed overnight and were able to get up, helped the nurses to put up the tree which the porters had delivered days before and which had been standing in a bucket of water in one of the sluices until there was time to deal with it.

The doctors' round was conducted with unusual informality, and lasted about half the usual time. Tony was distant and rather more reserved even than he normally was and Claire wondered why. His temper had indeed improved since he had met Fiona and Claire had got used to happier working relations with him on the unit. This morning, however, he was dour and cold and unresponsive to Claire's request for help with the decorations when the ward round ended.

So the nursing staff and the patients hung the tree with glass baubles, bells and stars and festooned it with 'angels' hair' before entwining red ribbons and tinsel around small bunches of holly and handing them up to a nurse on a chair who stuck one above the door into every cubicle on the unit. Before the morning was over, the unit was transformed.

Claire was grateful to be occupied all day. It stopped her from having to think about her own affairs. When Fiona rang her from theatre in the afternoon to tell her that she'd buy a tree on her way home as theatre had come to a standstill for the holiday, Claire cheerfully agreed. The evening would be passed in happy escapism too, and that suited Claire completely.

Tony disappeared after the ward round and had not appeared again by the time Claire went off duty. That was just as well, she reflected, as she changed into her outdoor clothes once more, as she had had a mad desire to ask the renal registrar whether he had seen his friend David Duncan lately. She was glad that no opportunity had presented itself for her to lay herself open to painful information. She did not want to know how he was avoiding seeing her or why. It was bad enough to come to her own uninformed and painful conclusion.

'Oh, it's lovely!' Claire exclaimed when she saw the little tree that Fiona had already put in a tub and decorated with red crêpe paper in the sitting-room of the flat.

Seeing her friend, Fiona immediately got up and went into the kitchen, returning with a glass.

'What's this?' Claire asked, surprised.

'Sherry. Cheers. Merry Christmas, Claire,' said Fiona holding her glass high.

'Cheers. How lovely,' Claire's heart lifted. She had soon got her coat off and was kneeling beside her flatmate on the carpet, patting down the earth around the base of the tree. Then they unpacked the decorations and got down to the serious business of decorating their own tree.

Claire stood up to survey their work and the envelope fell out of her pocket and landed on the floor beside where Fiona was kneeling.

Fiona picked it up to hand it to Claire.

'Here. Hey, that's David Duncan's writing,' she said.

'Yes,' said Claire dully. She took the letter that Fiona held up to her, the knowledge of its message an unwelcome intrusion into her evening.

'When did he write that?' Fiona asked. 'He's been off sick for three days. No sight or sound of him. Matthewson was not too well-pleased. He still doesn't seem to think he needs to let us know . . .' Fiona broke off what she was saying. 'What's up, Claire? What's wrong?'

'Nothing much. So he's ill?'

'Must be. Didn't you know? I assumed that you must know.'

'No,' said Claire slowly, 'I didn't know.'

Sue closed the door of the cubicle behind her and wished that the walls were not made of glass. She began, mechanically, to damp-dust the contents of the little room. She turned the mattress over on the bed, washed it and then turned her attention to the bedside locker. All the time she thought about Alan Foster, the patient who had occupied this room and whom she had 'lost'. Several times she had to stop because she could not see what she was doing for the tears that blurred her vision. This happened each time a new patient was to be admitted to 'his' bed, and Sue longed for this reaction of hers to fade away.

She wondered, not for the first time, why she had ever decided to become a nurse. Once, soon after she had come to work on the renal unit, and under circumstances not dissimilar from those under which she now worked, she had discussed this with Claire. They had decided that their reasons were similar: at least as a nurse you could do something, you could help. You did not have to suffer that dreaded, deadening feeling of helplessness that made the lot of relatives so unbearable.

Sue made a mental note to bring in some flowers from the nurses' station when she next came down the unit, to offset the austere presence of kidney machine and monitoring equipment in the waiting cubicle.

She had just got back to the station when the unit chief, Mr Schaffer, blew in with Humph trailing, like a battleship behind a tug, in his wake. Sue braced herself for the unknown. Mr Schaffer, tousled, distracted and with his coat done up on the wrong buttons as usual, looked at her as if he had never seen her before, in spite of the fact that she had finished conducting him on the ward round only an hour previously.

'Where's Sister?' he asked.

'She's on days off, Mr Schaffer,' Sue answered patiently, 'can I help you?'

'Now. It's the new admission. He's a surgeon here, in general theatre. He's on his way up from X-ray. I'll go over these notes with you.' Mr Schaffer stopped momentarily for breath, then ploughed on with his introductory remarks. Sue had to listen hard and long. Then the chief turned tail and flew out of the unit as if chased. He threw over his shoulder as he retreated a general remark to the effect that he expected the new patient to be in good hands. Sue smiled at Humph, who allowed herself the faintest glimmer of a smile in return.

'If he were coming on to an ordinary ward he'd be having a private room, of course,' said the Nursing Officer, sitting herself heavily down beside Sue at the desk and helping herself to a chocolate out of the box a relative had given to the nurses. 'So we'd better give him maximum privacy. I understand he knows all there is to know about his own condition, so maximum tact, and respect too. And he's refused a psychiatric assessment although he is a very over-anxious type. Just to let you in on the little details that the chief doesn't think worth telling you about.' Miss Humphreys patted her hair and took another chocolate.

'Thank you, Miss Humphreys. I'll try and treat him with the utmost respect. I hope we can do something for him.'

'And you'll be having the Christmas off, I hear?'

'That's right. I go off tomorrow . . . or rather, after this shift. Sister Brown is back tomorrow.'

'Well, some of us have to keep things going while you young ones enjoy yourselves,' Humph said in mock severity. 'Who did the tree?'

'Sister and the other nurses,' Sue said modestly, and took Humph's nod to mean approval.

'Call me if you need any help,' the Nursing Officer ordered, 'and if I don't see you before, Happy Christmas, Staff.'

'Thank you, Miss Humphreys, and the same to you,' Sue said. 'Do have a chocolate before you go.'

'Indeed I will,' said the Nursing Officer, and took another one to munch as she made her way out of the unit.

Fifteen minutes later a tall, angular man walked in through the swing doors. He was accompanied by Tony Fraser, who left him to approach the nurses' station alone while he disappeared into the doctors' room. The tall man gave Sue the impression that he had been much bigger, or would be if he had not been ill for some time. In his steely grey eyes she met the silent protest of his body against his sickness.

'Good morning,' he said quietly, 'I'm Dr David Duncan and I'm for admission to the unit. Mr Schaffer is expecting me.' He had with him a small suitcase which he now put down beside the desk.

'Good morning,' Sue said. 'The chief said he would be back shortly to see you, Dr Duncan. Meantime, I wonder if you would mind answering some questions for your nursing notesheet?'

With a resigned dispassion deeper than Sue had encountered before, Dr Duncan answered most of her questions. She took his closed attitude to be a bad omen for the future. You needed attack, vigour and determination to overcome renal disease; all qualities difficult to sustian through chronic illness. He had apparently sustained none of them. It worried Sue, but things could have been worse, she reflected as she showed him to his cubicle and screened it so that he could change, at least she did not know him and had never worked with him.

She had often thought how difficult it would be to nurse somebody with whom she had had a professional relationship before. It was hard enough when the relationship changed on to a personal basis from a purely working one. She thought of poor Sister and the registrar, Tony Fraser. It was awful to have to meet every day, talk together and then to have to spend the rest of the time trying to avoid one another because of what had happened between you outside work.

As far as Sue knew, Dr Duncan had only just come to work at St Helen's. She didn't recognise him from the dining-room, and neither did any of the students who were on with her this morning. It seemed he was new to the hospital, and Sue was glad of it. She had no preconceived ideas about what sort of person he was and neither did any of the staff on the unit as far as she knew. This would mean that they would easily be able to give him the respect and detached care that he deserved, just as if he were a lay person. In spite of what Humph had said, Sue firmly believed that all patients deserved the same treatment and she aimed to give it to each and every one of the patients who passed through her hands.

By the time Sue went off duty that afternoon the new patient had been seen by both the Unit Chief and the Registrar, who spent a great deal of the afternoon with him. He had been attached to the kidney machine in his room and was sitting up in bed reading as Sue went off duty, a strangely serious figure among the decorated cubicles and friendly occupants.

He looked up briefly as she passed his door on her way off the unit. She smiled in at him and asked if everything was all right. He thanked her stiffly and wished her a Happy Christmas, all without smiling. Sue waved cheerily and set her face forward. This was going to be the happiest Christmas of her life so far, and she was not going to let it be spoiled by reminders of a previous departure, a previous patient in this bed and a previous unhappy return to the renal unit.

Claire, refreshed after her days off, made mental notes of all the things that she wanted to do during the day as she walked through the colourful corridors of St Helen's on Christmas Eve morning. It was a habit that she had formed long ago and she did it almost unconsciously, so that however tired, taxed or preoccupied she was she arrived on duty with a clear idea of what she wanted to achieve that day, apart from the normal routine duties that her position demanded.

She was aware this morning that Christmas had its own unique dangers and drawbacks, both from the nurses' and from the patients' point of view. For the renal patients, many of whom were on strictly controlled diets which limited their intake of proteins, salts and liquids, there were the temptations of foods brought in by unwittingly kindly relatives, less familiar with their restrictions than they were themselves.

For the nurses, the emotional demands of Christmas, during which time they often supported both their own and their patient's loneliness and isolation, could prove too much. The tiredness that resulted could mean slips in professional competence, tearfulness, or forgetfulness. Relatives sometimes put an extra burden on nursing staff by expecting them to fulfill the role of the family for their particular relative whom they either could not, or did not want to visit over the holiday period; and there were a hundred other details which militated against calm care, all of which had a place in Claire's awareness. Her responsibility as sister of an effectively intensive care unit was even greater over these few days than it normally was.

It was small wonder, Claire reflected, that kidney failure patients were such 'difficult' patients sometimes. She felt that she would never be able to cope as they did with the struggle against their disease, week after week, month after month. She could not bear to return to a hospital every week for life-saving dialysis and to return home to listen for the telephone call that would tell them their kidney was waiting for them. Then face the post-operative wait to ensure that they had not rejected their transplant. She would not be able to bear it.

Claire reached the unit. She pushed open the swing doors and immediately noticed a crowd of people in the cubicle that had once been occupied by Alan Foster. Mr Schaffer was in there, as was the tall figure of Tony Fraser. There were two other white-coated figures, neither of whom she recognised, and an elderly gentleman of distinguished appearance who was soberly-suited and without a white coat. The doctors appeared to be deep in discussion. Claire could not see the new patient.

She walked briskly down the unit towards the station, nodding hellos and smiling at the patients as she passed them, and then, suddenly, as she drew level, she recognised David Duncan. He was already attached to his kidney machine, monitors faithfully recording his pulse, blood pressure, blood volume and so on. He was pale above the loose neck of his blue striped pyjamas.

Claire experienced one terrible controlled moment of truth, and then all was clear. Suddenly, everything that had happened to her in her life seemed to fall into place, to have meaning, to have equipped her to cope with this moment of realisation.

Whatever happened now, however cruel or kind fate was going to be to her, Claire felt she could play her part without hurting or failing David Duncan. It did not matter how his need expressed itself.

Claire did not interrupt the group of men around the bed of the new patient. She simply continued her journey to the station and sat down quietly beside Sue. She smiled at her colleague.

'You look exhausted,' she said sympathetically.

'I am,' Sue truthfully replied, 'I'll be glad of my holiday. It was the last minute rush. Everything was fairly quiet until eleven o'clock then Mrs Blair's shunt came out; Mrs McGregor's line got blocked and a drip almost ran through. We didn't know which way to run first. And then Tony rang up from Casualty to tell us that we'd be getting an emergency admission . . .'

'Oh, dear,' said Claire, 'and is that him?' She indicated Dr Duncan's cubicle. She felt her pulse race again as she put the question.

'Oh, no,' Sue replied quickly, 'that's yesterday's VIP admission. I was going to tell you about him first. He's the registrar, the new surgical registrar on the general theatre . . .'

Claire listened to the medical history of her new

patient with growing alarm and sickeningly familiar pessimism. It seemed that he had indeed been ill for as long as Tony had told her he had. It was all there in front of her in black and white: the early onset of his kidney disease, the struggle to qualify as a doctor, the worsening of his condition at around the time when she had first met him and, latterly, the twice-weekly journeys to another hospital to dialyse away from his place of work.

She saw that he had suddenly, and apparently violently, changed professional horses midstream, swapping a promising career in medicine for surgery after his senior housemanship. In a flash, Claire realised that the career ladder was quicker to climb in surgery; maybe he felt his time was limited.

Claire was glad to have a busy schedule in which to submerge herself, and, although she could not block out the gestures, movements and unknown words of the knot of people in David's cubicle, at least their presence there precluded her from having to make her visit to him under these new circumstances before she had herself got used to them. He must have had time to do so, she mused. How must he have felt, knowing that this was inevitable? Why hadn't he told her himself? She wished with all her heart that he had been able to find it in himself to share this with her sooner, and yet she understood why he could not.

She checked the documentation for the new admission mechanically but efficiently while her mind worked over and over instances, hints, snatches of conversation, fleeting expressions which she now felt should have given her a clue to his condition. Of all people, she had missed the tiny signs and symptoms which should have made all this plain to her before now. She could not believe that all the pieces of the puzzle had not fallen into place long ago.

Now she remembered his care in choosing his food,

his controlled intake of fluids. Now she recalled his irritability, his changes of moods and their superficiality. Suddenly she recalled his complaining of headache at least twice, and his refusal to give notice of illness at work was accounted for by the labile nature of his condition.

Claire caught herself beginning to blame herself for missing all these things, and yet she knew that she could not afford to do so. It would take all her power, professional and personal, to help David through this, and this she was determined to do. She must live, with him, for the day. Somehow, she must support him, at no matter what cost. It was the biggest, by far the greatest, challenge to her since she began her career as a nurse—and since she had become a woman.

Claire looked up from her paperwork to see the doctors streaming out of the cubicle which David now occupied, and coming towards her. Claire caught the confused expression on Tony's face and felt sorry for him. She wanted to let him know that she now understood his behaviour of the past weeks and yet there was no way she could do so quickly; no way that she could save him from the painful duty that he now faced.

Mr Schaffer caught Claire by the arm, although it was plain that she was waiting for him to address her.

'Sister, now where have you been? I'm leaving Dr Fraser here to acquaint you with the facts regarding our new patient and I trust you will respond in a suitable fashion to his presence in the unit. I'll be in and out. You're not going off again, Sister, are you?'

Claire was so used to her chief of medical staff by now that she barely noticed the curtness, the diffidence and the fatherly attitude he adopted towards her. He was a good doctor and that was all Claire cared about. She worked smoothly beside him and he trusted her totally, sometimes in preference to his junior medical staff when it came to astute observation and diagnosis. She, for her part, never abused his trust or allowed it to affect her respect for other members of the nursing and medical team on the unit.

'No, Mr Schaffer, I'm on over the Christmas period. Will you be in tomorrow? I'm sure we'd all be pleased to see you to wish you a Happy Christmas.'

Claire was briefly introduced to each of the doctors whom she did not know. The tall, distinguished gentleman turned out to be head of the tissue-typing department in Bristol with whom she knew Mr Schaffer was working closely on his transplant programme. It was a name she'd often heard and had never before been able to put a face to.

Then the senior men trailed out of the unit, talking as they went, Mr Schaffer bringing up the rear, having assured her that he would be in tomorrow, as usual on Christmas Day, probably with at least some of his six children in tow. They loved to come into the hospital. It was their special treat to come at Christmas and to visit not only the renal unit, but Mr Schaffer's smaller patients on the children's wards. Here they would share the fun, bringing their own special joy to the sick children at the same time.

Soon only Tony was left, facing Claire over the deserted nurses' station.

'I'm sorry, Claire,' he began.

'I'm sorry with you, Tony,' Claire said, softly.

'I was surprised that they admitted him to this unit. But the powers that be simply don't know everything, do they? I'm afraid it was a *fait accompli* as far as David was concerned. This was the nearest renal intensive care bed, and that was what he needed.'

'Yes. I see,' Claire said. 'Well, I for one, will make things as easy for him as I possibly can.' She looked up with frank eyes into those of the registrar.

'Good for you, Claire,' he gently said. 'That was how I thought you'd react.'

'Have you anything to tell me?' she asked in professional tones, 'because when you've given me the information that I need I shall go and speak to him.'

'Go now,' Tony said. 'We can go over one or two things in my room later. I don't want him to think we're talking about him endlessly here.'

Claire nodded her agreement. It was some small compensation for the circumstances under which they now found themselves working that the relationship between them had magically reverted to its former easiness.

Claire also instinctively knew that she must avoid over-nursing David; that to pay him too much attention would be worse than to pay him none at all. The most important thing was to work quietly and determinedly to restore his physical strength and his psychological fitness for whatever treatment would be his. Claire had cared for kidney patients for long enough to understand fully and never to underestimate the effect of the mental attitude of the patient on the success or failure of their treatment, whether it be dialysis or a kidney transplant.

So she left it some time before she entered the silent cubicle where the surgical registrar was reading. She also timed her entrance to coincide with that of a staff nurse who was recording routine observations of temperature and pulse and checking the monitors in the room.

'Good afternoon, Dr Duncan,' she said. He looked up. He was caught off-guard.

'Good afternoon,' he returned, his voice edged with something . . . pain?

The staff nurse finished writing on a chart and put it neatly down on the pile beside the kidney machine. Claire picked it up again and noted the steady observations with satisfaction.

'Just finished, Sister,' the staff nurse smiled at her.

'If you've got nothing else to do, why don't you go off, Staff? And take the rest of the early shift off with you.'

'Thank you very much, Sister. See you tomorrow morning, then.' The girl went out, closing the glass door softly behind her.

'I'm sorry . . .' Claire began, tidying the locker top, not looking directly at him.

'Don't be sorry for me,' Dr Duncan's voice surprised her with its fullness and its firmness. She looked at his face and found the chin set and the mouth hard, courage and unmistakable pride in the grey eyes. 'For God's sake, call me an unlucky bastard if you want to, but don't feel sorry for me.'

Claire was shaken to the core by his words. They echoed like an iron bell chiming in her head.

'I didn't mean that, David,' she said, at last, 'I do not feel sorry for you.' Her voice was firmer than she could have believed it could be.

'Thank God for that,' he replied under his breath.

'It is not my fault that you are here, David,' Claire said carefully, controlling her voice.

'It isn't mine either. I can assure you that this is the last place on earth that I wanted to land up,' David Duncan looked at Claire, his face flushed with anger, his eyes icy.

'I can believe that,' she said, softly. 'That was what I meant when I said I was sorry.'

He regarded her steadily, but his knuckles showed less white as he grasped the book he had been reading, and Claire hoped that he accepted her words. They had been sincere enough.

The hospital chapel was decorated for Christmas with pyramids of holly, ivy and mistletoe beside the aisle and a great bowl of white lilies underneath the tall lectern. The foliage and flowers gave off a deep, earthy smell that reminded Claire of the park in autumn. The chapel, tiny as it was and set in the heart of the hospital, beat with its own private life, hope and peace, and provided a haven for all who entered it.

It was treated as a local church by the many nurses who lived in and who worshipped there every Sunday at services organised by the hospital chaplain. It was loved as a tranquil, private retreat by many nurses and doctors who came there to think, away from the bustle and intrusion of the rest of the hospital. And it was a sanctuary for relatives and friends of patients who came to pray, to weep or to give thanks.

This Christmas Eve evening the chapel was filled with the subdued voices of red-cloaked nurses gathering together before going carol singing around St Helen's. There were already almost twenty when Claire arrived and she represented one of the last to join the band. She had been late coming off duty.

Claire's eyes wandered around the group as she listened to the instructions of the girl in charge. And then she noticed an elderly woman sitting at the front of the chapel, her back to the carol singers. She was so still that she might have been a statue. She was wearing a tweed coat and a coloured scarf around her neck, but her head of thick grey hair was bare, and shone in the candlelight. She seemed to be looking at the altar. She did not adopt the attitude of one praying. Claire imagined that her eyes were open, and there was something about the woman which Claire recognised.

She asked the girl standing next to her to collect a song sheet on her behalf and moved away from the knot of nurses, down the central aisle of the chapel until she drew level with the woman in the front pew. It was the same person whom she had seen visit Dr Duncan earlier that evening. Claire passed quickly by the seated figure and along the other side of the front row, intending to rejoin her singing colleagues at the door of the chapel, but she found a light hand on her arm restraining her.

Looking down she saw the face of Mrs Duncan. The grey eyes that met hers were troubled, but passionate. They wore an expression that Claire had met before in another's eyes. The strangely familiar face was composed.

'Sister Brown?' the woman asked. Her voice was cultured and bore just a trace of the Scottish lilt that her son had also retained.

'Yes,' Claire confirmed. 'I'm Sister Brown.'

'I am the mother of Dr David Duncan,' the woman softly intoned. 'I hoped to speak to you earlier on the unit, but I had to hurry away. The medical staff wanted to talk with my son and you were busy elsewhere.'

'How do you do, Mrs Duncan,' Claire said. 'I am so sorry. I should have introduced myself to you earlier, on the unit. I hope you are not too concerned about your son, Mrs Duncan. We shall do all as we possibly can for him, you know.'

The older woman looked at Claire with kindness and compassion, as if, Claire felt, their positions were reversed.

'Oh, I know you will, Sister Brown. I have been through a great deal down the years that David has been ill, and I am quite prepared for anything that might happen. And you had no need to introduce yourself to me, Sister, I knew quite well who you were. David has talked about you often enough to me.'

Claire's heart stopped. The murmur of voices reached her from the nurses, a vague reminder that they were waiting for her to rejoin them before setting off around the hospital. The smell of the holly and ivy bathed her senses, and for a long unearthly moment she thought she must be dreaming. But she was not dreaming.

Mrs Duncan was doing up the buttons on her coat. She

held out her hand formally to Claire and Claire took it.

'It is nice to meet you, Mrs Duncan,' she said.

'And you too, dear,' the woman replied, her voice warm, 'Happy Christmas.'

'The same to you,' Claire said.

The two women walked quickly down the chapel away from the altar. Mrs Duncan arranged her scarf as she walked away, down the long corridor to the outside world. Claire pulled her red cape around her and rejoined her colleagues.

CHAPTER SIX

CLAIRE put Sue in charge of the care of Dr Duncan as soon as she returned from her Christmas holiday. At the same time, Claire wondered what sort of ill fate had made her so keen for Sue to go away on a management course so soon after Christmas. It meant that she could not keep out of David's professional care forever.

She already saw him several times a day, but these visits were supervisory and therefore not concerned with his intimate care, a thing with which she dreaded becoming involved, for both their sakes.

Dr Duncan remained aloof and unapproachable. He returned her formal daily greetings and exchanged small talk about the weather. Further than this he did not go, and Claire did not venture. Several times she admitted his mother at visiting times; always dignified, serious and polite. But Mrs Duncan did not ever ask to speak to her alone, or enquire of her as to her son's health, or make any personal comment to her again.

Sue, upon her return to work, looked radiant.

'I don't have to ask you what sort of Christmas you had!' Claire exclaimed, as the staff nurse walked up to the nurses' station, smiling, her hair glossy and her whole demeanour relaxed and contented.

'No,' she said, 'but if you do, I should have to say, smashing.' She grinned at Claire.

'Even the in-laws?' Claire asked. They had had a discussion about mother-in-laws and their reputation before Sue had gone off on holiday. They had wondered whether mother-in-laws deserved their bad name from the outset, or whether they rightfully acquired it. When

118

did they change into dragons from the sweet and approving mother of the boyfriend? At the wedding ceremony, at the reception or after the birth of the first grandchild, they had wondered.

'Groundless worries,' Sue now assured Claire. 'She is as lovely now as she was before we got married. Honestly, it was a super Christmas. What was it like here?'

'Take a deep breath,' Claire said, 'we've had three new admissions and that doesn't include Dr Duncan, whom you admitted. So we've been pretty busy . . .'

'How is he?' Sue interrupted, 'Dr Duncan, I mean.'

'He's pretty low. He's been the same ever since I came back from my days off before Christmas. He is dialysing every day for four hours and he seems to take that in his stride. But his general mood is low. Sue, I'm sorry to have to put this on you the minute you get back, and I know the implications that particular room has for you, but I want to ask you to take special responsibility for him. Until you go off on your course, that is.'

'Oh, Lord,' Sue groaned, 'I'd completely forgotten the course. Yes, of course I'll look after Dr Duncan. In fact, I'd rather look after the most bolshie patient for a year at a time than go on a management course . . . and he's quite good-looking in a dour sort of way . . .'

Claire smiled. She longed to confide in Sue and yet she knew her control depended upon the complete secrecy of her feelings in regard to Dr Duncan.

Claire also secretly understood exactly what Sue meant about the course. But she was being cruel in order to be kind. Sue would never have put herself forward for it, and it was up to Claire to release her and to encourage her to equip herself for promotion at this stage in her career. Sue was so preoccupied with her new marriage, her husband and her new home, that the position that she currently held on the kidney unit was more than enough for her professionally. She was in no mental state to look into the future at the moment, but Claire felt that the time would almost certainly come for her when she would be glad that she'd spent that short week learning the basics of management with a group of nurses of her own age and experience.

Sue adopted the bantering, gentle bullying technique with David that she had used when she looked after poor Alan in the very same cubicle. Once Claire interrupted Sue going back into David's room with a drink of what looked like raspberry milkshake.

'What on earth's that?' Claire asked. It was afternoon tea-time and all the other patients were nibbling sandwiches and drinking tea.

'Lord Duncan says that if I bring him any more of that salt-free bread he'll do something rather unpleasant with it—and me,' she laughed. 'So this is a high calorie drink instead. He says he prefers it.'

Claire looked into the cubicle and noticed that David was studiously reading, trying not to notice them talking outside his room. She felt a rush of mixed emotions as Sue went in with the drink.

Claire went to her sitting-room, closed the door and made herself a cup of coffee. Tomorrow was Sue's last day before she went off on her course, and Claire found herself glad of this. She mentally rejected the idea that she could possibly be jealous of Sue and David getting on so well—yet her emotions told her that she was.

She made her cup of instant coffee blacker than usual and stood, with shaking hands, drinking it beside her desk. What a mess her life was in. She cared about him so deeply and he rejected her so completely. She did not know for how much longer she could bear her feelings, and yet she knew that she could not stop feeling them.

At that moment there was a light tap on the door. Mechanically, Claire called 'come in', and Tony entered

the room. He was dressed in slacks and a tweed jacket
and was obviously on his way off the unit.

'God, you look awful,' he said, 'any chance of coffee?'

'Thank you very much,' Claire said. 'Yes, make yourself one.'

'Well?' Tony crossed to the small table and put the
kettle on to boil again.

'Will you make me another cup too, please?' Claire
returned, not looking at him.

He came over and took her cup gently out of her hand.

'Poor old Claire,' he said.

'What do you mean? Poor old me?' Claire turned on
him, surprised at her own anger and at the tears that
were hot, leaden behind her lids.

'Just what I say,' Tony quietly repeated his words.

Claire stood numb, unable to move although she
knew that she should sit down.

Tony walked across with the two cups of coffee he'd
made and put them both down on Claire's desk. Then he
slowly and firmly took her by the shoulders and held her
to face him for a long moment. Before she knew what
had moved her she was in his arms, sobbing, unable to
catch her breath and she could feel his warm breath in
her hair. He held her tightly, only letting her go when
her sobs ceased and she managed to surface from the
depths of her misery.

'I'm so sorry, Tony . . .' she gasped, searching in her
dress pocket for a tissue.

'It's okay, Claire, you don't have to apologise. We're
in this together, you know. Here, sit down and take this,'
he handed her her coffee.

Claire composed herself.

'I can't help him,' she said, staring at Tony with all the
distraction that she felt reflected in her eyes. 'He hates
me to go near him.'

'How would you feel, Claire? He doesn't hate you, in

any way . . .' Tony's voice trailed off and then came back again, sure and strong, 'but he hates the way he is . . . now . . .'

'Yes. I understand that. But if he only knew that I don't just see his body lying there . . .' Claire broke off, suddenly shocked at her confiding in the registrar. How could she explain to anyone how much she cared for Dr Duncan's mind and his feelings and how much she longed for that to be reciprocated. It seemed that men only understood the language of the body; physical love. And yet here was Tony, being kind and tender towards her as he had never been before. Everything seemed to happen in the wrong order, with the wrong people, at the wrong times.

'He probably does understand that, Claire. But he feels . . . he feels like an animal . . . he feels at a disadvantage,' he finished lamely.

Claire looked at the registrar. She felt as if she had known him for many more than the two years that they had now been working together on the kidney unit. She was suddenly overwhelmingly touched that he could show her such kindness.

'I do understand,' she returned, closing the conversation, stopping him from having to make any more excuses for his friend. 'Are you off now?' she added.

'Yes. I'm going to drive to Bristol to the tissue-typing lab. and then, this evening, I'm taking your flatmate out, probably to the cinema. Why don't you join us, Claire?'

'That's really sweet of you, Tony, but no thanks. I really don't fancy the role of gooseberry!' she hoped this did not sound too ungracious, because it was the truth.

'Okay. So you won't come with us this evening. It's okay, Claire. I'll see you tomorrow.'

'Yes, Tony,' Claire said softly, and the door closed behind him, leaving her in welcome peace and quiet.

She realised that it was past four-thirty and that she

should be thinking about going off duty herself, she thought she would just tell Sue that she was off, change and walk back to the flat. The fresh air would be welcome this afternoon.

There was another tap on the door and Claire braced herself subconsciously for the re-entry of Tony. But it was Sue.

'Ah, Sister, Claire, I mean. I'm glad you haven't gone off already. I thought I might have missed you. I wondered what you were going to do this evening. Only, we wondered if you'd like to come and have a meal with us. If you're not doing anything, that is.'

Claire looked up gratefully at the staff nurse. She seemed like an angel, heaven-sent. There was nothing that Claire felt would be nicer to do this evening. She had never been to Sue's new house, although she knew vaguely where it was.

'I'd love that, Sue,' she said.

'Oh, good,' Sue responded. 'Have you got the address? If you catch a 99 bus and get off at the cricket pitch, it's two minutes' walk from there.'

'Lovely. When shall I come?' Claire asked.

At seven o'clock that evening she got off the bus and followed the directions that she'd been given into the neat street of new, semi-detached houses. The small front garden of number ten was screened from the road by a privet hedge and from the path Claire could see into the big, spacious living-room at the front of the house.

Later, saying goodbye to Sue and John in the curtained sitting-room that contained their warm, safe love, Claire thought that it must all be worth the difficulties and troubles that beset every relationship. It would be worth all the agony she'd been through on his behalf to have David walking beside her now down the garden path and homewards, to feel the warmth and safety of his strong hand in hers, his arm around her shoulders. She shuddered as she imagined his voice, close to her ear, his lips brushing her hair, the safe masculine protection of his presence.

But, when they had been together it had not been all sweetness and tenderness. It had been hard, brutal love-making; everything that she had ever dreaded with a man. He had not spoken softly, or looked tenderly at her, and yet she had accepted him, longing for the old David Duncan while melting into the passionate embraces of this new, unknown character as if her very body had its own will, independent of her mind.

A bus drew up and she boarded it. It was full of teenagers, some sitting close together on the back seat in silent, inexpert embraces; some giggling together, sitting back to front in their seats. All of them represented to Claire the abandon of youth and the enthusiasm of young love. Their joy made Claire retreat even further into herself.

If only he would give her some sign. If only there would be a letter or note sent to the flat. She could understand why he avoided contact with her on the unit. But there were other ways. He must know that it was as hard for her as it was for him, this situation. And yet he gave her nothing to believe in; no encouragement.

By the time she got to the flat she had almost convinced herself that there might be a message; she had almost willed there to be one. But the flat was in darkness. Even Fiona was not back yet. It was midnight. The only envelope on the mantelpiece was a buff coloured one from the tax people.

Claire went to bed and tried to sleep. But sleep would not come.

'How are you getting along with your VIP, Sister?' It was Miss Humphreys. She was due for a round of the unit, but as far as Claire was concerned she could not have turned up at a more inconvenient moment. Sue was off on her course. There were two new students on the unit, neither of whom had done any intensive care nursing up until now, and the staff nurses were both on late. Claire had to make this morning one continuous teaching session. She had eight full beds, and the prospect did not please her.

There was no real chance of allocating one patient to each nurse—her preferred arrangement—and it was just as well that only one of the patients was very ill. That one really demanded all Claire's attention, as the most senior nurse, and that patient was David Duncan. He was very weak and, in Claire's judgment, needed a special nurse allocated to him alone.

The staff nurse with whom Claire should have been on this morning had 'phoned to say that she was sick and did not feel able to come on duty; the relatives of an outpatient had just 'phoned to ask if he could arrive later for his dialysis and three lots of drip fluid were all about to run through simultaneously.

'I'd like to speak to you about Dr Duncan, Miss Humphreys,' Claire told the Nursing Officer, 'but could you possibly wait a moment?'

She summoned the terrified students and quickly identified the most senior one by her uniform stripes.

'Nurse, I'd like you to take both your colleagues and show them how to change the drips on the patients in cubicles three, four and seven. You can bring me the charts and new bottles so that I can check with you that they're the right ones. That's the most urgent task. After that we can think again about your mornings. All right?'

'Yes, Sister.' The oldest student nurse looked competent enough, it was a task well within her ability and one which she felt safe with, even in this new, alien environment.

As they followed one another into the first cubicle, Claire turned back to the Nursing Officer.

'All new this morning,' she explained. 'And the staff nurse's off sick.'

'And the doctor needs specialling?' Miss Humphreys took in the situation at a glance.

'Yes. He does, really. Is it possible?' Claire asked. She knew that the Nursing Officer's job entailed constant shuffling and reshuffling of wholly inadequate numbers of nursing staff.

'Did you have the Wilson girl one day last week? The one that's just back from the intensive care course?' she asked Claire.

Claire had a flashing memory of an efficient, red-headed girl who had specialled a patient for her for a day and impressed her in the process.

'Yes, I believe I did,' she said.

'She's relieving on male surgical. I'll send her over to you,' the Nursing Officer briskly announced. 'And I'll come back later for the round. Give you time to sort yourself out.' She thundered out of the unit before Claire had time to thank her.

The Nursing Officer was as good as her word. Within ten minutes, the auburn-haired staff nurse had presented herself to Claire on the unit, had gone over the nursing notes for Dr Duncan and was at his bedside. Claire felt she could relax.

She spent the next hour with the student nurses, orientating them to the awesome kidney unit, introducing them to the patients and to the equipment upon which their lives depended.

But the moment soon arrived when Claire found she must relieve the staff nurse who was specialling David, sending her off for an early lunch along with the most junior student nurse. The others could cope with the routine work until the afternoon shift arrived and took over at one-thirty.

The red-haired staff nurse calmly indicated to Claire her observations over the past two-and-a-half hours and Claire noted the slight temperature spike which had appeared an hour earlier. The pulse rate was only very slightly elevated, but Claire feared the possible onset of an infection.

When the nurse had gone she gently, without waking the sleeping patient, removed the bandage and dressing from the shunt site on Dr Duncan's wrist. Sure enough, there on either side of the silastic tube 'bridge' that ran between the artery and the vein and gave access to his circulation for the connection to a kidney machine, the skin was red and angry looking.

Claire had dreaded this. Dr Duncan was rapidly running out of suitable sites for a shunt as many of these had been used and reused over the years, causing the vessels to collapse and be rendered useless. Tony had reckoned himself lucky to get this site working, and now it looked as if there was infection here too. The tissue would break down quickly, it was already so fragile.

She was still examining the sore, puckered skin and was about to take a swab for bacteriology, when David Duncan opened his eyes.

'What the hell are you doing? What's going on?' he said. But he was not stupid enough to pull his arm away from Claire's firm but gentle professional hold.

'I think the shunt's infected,' Claire told him bluntly. 'But not too badly. I don't think it'll have to come out.'

'Take a swab then,' he told her gruffly.

'I have. Thank you,' she replied rather curtly.

He looked at her with hostility.

'Where's Staff?' he asked next.

'At lunch,' Claire replied, just as shortly.

'She coming back?'

Claire nodded, involved in her work.

He watched as she replaced the dressing on his shunt site.

Eventually he said, 'I know, I know. I didn't mean anything. She's a good nurse,' he added as an explanatory afterthought.

Claire felt anger rising inside her.

'Most of us are,' she told him.

'I'm a waste of your time,' Dr Duncan stated. His voice was cold and his face betrayed no emotion.

Claire felt her heart sink. This kind of talk was dangerous. For him it was dangerous because it undermined his own belief in himself; for her it could lead to the downfall of her professional control of the situation. Claire took a deep breath.

'I don't want to hear that from you,' she said, very quietly, very calmly. She went to the bed and stood looking into his eyes, refusing to be repelled by their icy regard. 'I never, ever want to hear that from you again. You are going to get better, Dr Duncan. You are going to walk out of this unit a fit man with a healthy future ahead of you. And you are going to continue your career, walk in summer fields, eat your mother's good food again and, and . . .' Claire paused, her heart in her mouth, '. . . and anything else that you want out of life, you are going to have. Do you understand that, Dr Duncan?'

Something happened in the grey eyes; a flicker, a light which, once lit, continued to burn there. He held her gaze steadily. The moment seemed to last forever and nothing else existed in it but this coming together. Claire could hear her own heartbeat. At last she tore her eyes away. She picked up the stethoscope which hung behind Dr Duncan's bed and mechanically attached it to the wall sphygmomonometer. She recorded his blood pressure, then his pulse and then took his temperature. It continued to rise. It was up by point four of a degree on the previous recording. Claire made notes of everything she had done for him.

The staff nurse returned quietly from her lunch and reported straight back to the cubicle to relieve Claire.

'I've taken a swab,' she told the girl. 'The temp's up a bit further, but Dr Duncan is comfortable. I'll pop back in to see how things are going as soon as I get back from lunch. Thanks, Staff.'

'You've done the one o'clock observations. Thank you, Sister.'

Dr Fraser looked up quickly from the pile of casenotes he was working on as Claire entered the room.

'Oh, dear,' he said, seeing the specimen that she carried, 'my least favourite sight is the vision of you with a swab full of bad news. Whose is that?'

'It's from David Duncan's shunt site. His temp. is up a bit and the area around the shunt is inflamed. Still, perhaps we've caught the infection soon enough to stop it doing any harm.'

'I hope so,' Tony answered.

'There's nowhere else to put a shunt if this one has to come out, is there?'

'In simple terms—no. There isn't. Nowhere easy, anyway.'

'I'll send this off by special messenger to bacteriology and we'll just have to hope that we've caught it in time.'

'Thank you, Claire. I'll start him on a broad spectrum antibiotic until I know what the sensitivities are,' Tony frowned and ran his hand over his forehead in a worried gesture.

'Is he waiting for a transplant, Tony?' Claire asked, as casually as she could. There had been no mention of David being on a waiting list for a donor kidney.

'He's been on the list for a year,' Tony told Claire, 'but his tissue-type is fairly rare. No brothers or sisters, and his only parent is too old to donate a kidney. So that seems to be that.'

Claire tried to adjust herself to the facts. If anything happened to Dr Duncan's lifeline by which he was attached to the kidney machine, he could die. His only real, lasting chance was a transplant, and there had been no success in finding a kidney for him up until now. And time was running out. The longer he remained dependent on the kidney machine the weaker he became. He had gone past the stage of being well controlled on dialysis physically and, more importantly, psychologically. He had given up hope for himself.

The infection did get worse before it got better, but three days later Claire felt more optimistic when Tony handed her the lab. reports on the latest swab taken from the infected area. Dr Duncan seemed to be mending.

Claire went into the cubicle. The red-haired staff nurse was still specialling-him and David Duncan was sitting up, immersed in a book.

'Hello, Sister,' the staff nurse greeted Claire, handing her the charts that she had just finished marking up for the last set of observations. Dr Duncan looked up from his book and regarded Claire as she expertly scanned the recordings, before looking back at his book again.

To her relief, the temperature had dropped to thirty-eight degrees centigrade; only one degree above normal. With the help of his four-hourly injections of antibiotics he seemed to be winning the battle against his infection.

'How are you feeling, Dr Duncan?' Claire asked, very aware of the presence of the staff nurse.

'Much better, thank you, Sister,' he responded politely.

'Your temperature is down,' Claire informed him.

'Yes. Staff Nurse told me that it was,' he said. He

seemed to view all that happened to him nowadays with a sort of distance, as if it wasn't happening to his own body. It was a denial of his illness that expressed itself in uninterest.

'Good news,' Claire persevered brightly.

Dr Duncan looked straight at Claire with barely veiled anger.

'If you say so, Sister,' he said.

Claire turned abruptly and left the cubicle, feeling disturbed and unsettled.

She had heard from the other patients of David's age about their largely unsuccessful attempts at 'getting through' to the surgeon. Dr Duncan had rejected all friendly advances and seemed to be happy to be left alone. Even the visits from his mother seemed to have become less frequent. Dr Duncan was cutting himself off from everybody, carefully and systematically retreating into himself.

It was half past three in the afternoon and the patients were just finishing their tea when the red alarm bell at the nurses' station rang and Claire saw, with a kind of cold horror, that it was above David Duncan's cubicle on her indicator panel.

She was there before she'd had time to think, and the dreadful truth hit her at once. David Duncan's tubing had become disconnected at the shunt site and he was losing blood at an alarming rate.

The staff nurse was applying pressure and Claire automatically reached for the two clips which were out of her reach as she was using both hands. She clipped off the two bleeding points and staunched the flow. But he had already lost a lot of blood.

The staff nurse did not even take time to rinse her hands before taking his blood pressure, which was very low. Claire helped her to elevate the end of the bed and then went to find Tony. She had to ring for him. It was a

Sunday afternoon and he was on call from the residency. Within ten minutes he was on the unit, pale, anxious and obviously very tense.

Claire gave him a swift run-down on what had happened. By the time they got back to his bedside, David Duncan had slipped into unconsciousness, but his vital signs were stronger than they had been a few minutes before. Together, the staff nurse and Claire changed the bed and made the patient as comfortable as they could, while Tony put up a drip and sent for blood from the blood transfusion department.

Two hours later, Claire went off duty, trembling with tiredness and emotional exhaustion. She had felt David's cold, clammy forehead and had an unforgettable mental image of the closed eyes that seemed never to want to open again. She could not get away from that last glimpse of her patient before she eventually left the unit. Tony had shaken his head over the shunt. They would try to repair it this evening.

It was very rare for tubing to come apart as this had done, but it could do so, especially after an infection at the site. Nothing seemed to be going right for David, and Claire found herself increasingly unable to keep up a cheerful face for him.

'It seems quite incredible,' Mr Schaffer was saying, 'that with the international net flung so wide we still can't find kidneys for people like this . . .'

Claire had come in on the end of what had obviously been an important ward round. The medical staff were still clustered in a tight knot outside David Duncan's room, talking in hushed voices, and Claire had to excuse herself and walk through them to get from the corridor to the station.

Fiona was going out with Tony Fraser tonight, she had told Claire, as they had had to cancel their date over the weekend due to some emergency theatre cases he'd had to take. Claire had not explained about David, or told Fiona that it was he who had been the cause of her lost evening with Tony Fraser. For a start it was unethical to discuss cases outside the unit, and for another, it would have caused her much more pain than she liked to admit to have to talk about it with Fiona. She was nursing her anxiety over David Duncan in her own private hell.

Among the doctors in the corridor was the tall distinguished looking man from the transplant centre at Bristol. It was not usual for him to be on the unit, let alone on a ward round.

As Claire drew near she heard him saying, 'Purely a matter of luck . . .' He drew in his breath and then held it for what seemed ages. Then he shrugged, 'I suppose we could go through the results of all the tissue-typing we did on ourselves,' he said thoughtfully. 'Obviously a very long shot. But then, why not?'

In a flash, Claire realised that they had been discussing David and that they'd reached the conclusion that a transplant was his only hope. She could see the surgeon lying asleep. The same staff nurse who had been looking after him for a week was taking his pulse and counting his respirations at the same time.

'A very long shot indeed . . .' Mr Schaffer was saying, uncertainly, 'Still, if you think it's worth a go, old man.'

Claire could see the tension in Tony Fraser's face as he listened to the senior men juggling their ideas. She knew how profoundly their decision was going to affect Tony personally and that this was the first time anything like this had happened to him during his professional life.

It was not until two hours later that Claire had a chance to talk to him. She went quietly into the doctors' room and closed the door behind her. Tony was looking out of the window on to the windy, rainswept quadrangle. The weather had suddenly thawed and the rain fallen, driven by gusty, warm, west winds.

'Tony?' she ventured. She was still standing just inside the doorway, unsure of the registrar's mood. He turned round to face her and she saw how thrown he was from his normal easy-going manner. His face seemed to have set hard into a similar stony attitude as that worn by his close friend David Duncan.

'I couldn't help hearing . . .' Claire began, '. . . on the round.' She broke off, uncertain how to tackle him.

'It's a last ditch attempt,' the registrar said at last. 'If we don't find him a kidney soon, very soon, it'll be too late to save him.'

Claire swallowed, shocked at the finality of the registrar's words.

'Tony,' she said, very softly. 'I want you to do something for me.'

'What's that?' he asked, dully.

'Do you remember, in the Lakes, you said something about live donors and about needing volunteers for the project? Well, I want you to try me. Will you, please, Tony?'

Claire was unaware of the urgency in her voice. She was only aware of her feelings and of her burning desire for Tony to accept her request.

'Are you serious?' Tony asked, incredulously.

Claire nodded.

'I have never been more serious,' she replied.

'Of course,' Tony said in a tired voice, articulating his thoughts rather than addressing Claire directly, 'there is virtually no chance of our finding a kidney compatible with his tissue-type in time, and so, why not try anything . . .'

Claire willed Tony's attention back to herself.

'Well?' she persisted.

'You really want to be tissue-typed?' Tony repeated.

'Yes,' Claire said.

'You are a very remarkable person, Claire, and David is a lucky man . . .'

'When will you do the tests?' Claire asked quickly.

'I can take the blood today and send the sample off with the chaps from Bristol this afternoon. Quicker than the messenger,' Tony responded, almost absent-mindedly.

'Fine,' Claire replied.

It was not until she was on her way home through the dark streets of Elchester, that Tony's exhausted expression and his words came back to Claire with a clarity that she had not experienced at the time. She could not help wondering what sort of an evening he and Fiona had or were having. She could not imagine him being very good company in his present state of anxiety over David. But at least he and Fiona had a date.

Tired and worried as she was, Claire found herself wondering bitterly whether her life was destined to be lived as a nurse and friend. And what had Tony meant by the back-handed compliment implied in the remark about his friend being a 'lucky man'? By no stretch of the imagination could this description fit Dr David Duncan. Yet Claire wished that she could believe that he did indeed value her care, even if only professionally. Instead, he seemed to deny her the only encouragement that really meant anything to her, and compliments from others had a hollow ring as a result.

She had to find strength within herself to cope with the future and anything that it might hold, but of one thing she remained certain, she did not want to lose David Duncan and she would do all she humanly could to save him.

CHAPTER SEVEN

CLAIRE stood, hardly daring to breathe, watching the sleeping surgeon. She knew that when his eyes opened she would be plunged into the most difficult encounter of her life. Dr Duncan was to undergo transplant surgery in two days' time and the new kidney he would receive would be one of her own.

The last two weeks had passed in a dream-like state for Claire: there had been Mr Schaffer's amazed, grave announcement that the kidney matched and that Claire's tissue type was extremely close to that of the surgeon, and then Tony's long talk with her, going over all the implications, both surgical and social, of her decision.

Fiona had been marvellously supportive once she had got over the shock of hearing of Claire's intention. Claire did not know that her flatmate had, at the outset, tried to persuade Tony to put Claire off the idea of offering such dramatic help, but that Tony had been far too concerned for David Duncan to try to do so. Instead Tony had treated Claire with the deep admiration and concern which he genuinely felt and he had promised her that he would do all in his power to make her operation a success. The two of them were now bound together inextricably in their undertaking to save Dr Duncan's life.

It was not a new partnership. It seemed almost a natural extension of the working relationship that they had built up during their time together on the Kidney Unit. Both Claire and Tony knew what they had to do and what was at stake. It seemed that Fiona faced the most difficult task in accepting the situation.

Only the most senior nursing and medical staff in the unit and hospital knew that Claire was to donate her kidney and discreet arrangements had been made for her care in a side-ward on the surgical ward nearby. As far as the staff on the Kidney Unit were concerned, Sister was going off for three weeks' holiday from that afternoon and this was the information that Claire had come to impart to Dr Duncan.

Her heart stopped as a frown flickered over the sleeping features before her, and then the eyes opened and she met their icy stare. She had been lulled into calm by the comparative composure of Dr Duncan's sleeping face, and now the shock of his obvious displeasure at her presence made Claire feel momentarily faint.

The surgeon brought himself up into a sitting position with a single movement of his broad shoulders, a movement which belied his weak physical condition.

'What do you want, Sister?' He almost spat her title at her.

Claire took a deep breath.

'How are you feeling, Dr Duncan?' she asked in quiet, professional tones, ignoring the venom in his voice.

'Great,' replied the surgeon, the irony of his remark underlined by a twisted smile.

'That was not supposed to be a cliché,' Claire persisted, 'I wondered how you were feeling about your surgery.'

'Oh, did you?' Dr Duncan responded. He raised his eyebrows in an expression of mock interest. Beyond the pain of his cruelty towards her, Claire was aware of the symmetry of the fine eyes and of their heart-stopping clarity. She felt as though she was doomed never to look into those eyes again without meeting their owner's contempt for her.

'How do you feel about it, 'Dr Duncan?' she persisted, 'Perhaps I could find someone with whom you would like to discuss it, apart from the unit staff, I mean?' she offered.

'Oh, God, I do wish you would leave me alone. I don't need your routine care and concern, Sister Brown. I don't want to discuss anything with you. I am in full possession of the facts and can cope with them perfectly well.' He paused. 'Thank you, all the same,' he finished wearily, dismissively.

'That's not good enough, Dr Duncan,' Claire said, still in a quiet, sure voice. 'We need your help as much as you need ours. More than half the will for your recovery has to come from inside you . . .'

Claire was stopped by the flush of fury that she saw flood the surgeon's face. The look of hatred that he threw at her filled her with cold dread.

'Will you stop it, Sister? Or shall I get up and leave the room.'

Claire suddenly realised that she would not be able to restrain him from such an act and that he would not accept any more pressure from her. Even in his current physical and mental state he was stronger, much stronger than she was. She had no influence over him. She had admit her failure to will into him a desire to live.

She met the cold, stranger's look that he gave her.

'I wanted you to know,' she began, and he sighed openly at her new attempt to communicate with him. 'I wanted you to know that I'll be away for the next three weeks, so Staff Nurse Craig will be in charge of the Renal Unit and your care. Any special demands that you may have can be dealt with by her . . .'

Claire sensed an almost tangible relaxation in the man before her. At the same time there was a momentary softening of the expression in his eyes. So it was a relief for him to know that she would not be here to see; to look after him; to watch him recovering. Claire could not bear to pursue the thought.

'Enjoy yourself,' he remarked flippantly.

'Good luck, Dr Duncan,' Claire said, her voice barely audible.

As she turned to leave the room she felt his eyes following her, the intensity of his stare burning into her.

'Yes,' he muttered, and then, under his breath, 'Good luck to you too.' There was no sarcasm in his final words to her.

Claire had reached the door to the corridor but she heard his last remark with a shock. He had not been told who the donor was to be. Tony had promised her faithfully that her identity would remain a secret from Dr Duncan even though he would know by now that the donor of his new kidney was to be a live one. The remark could only mean that the surgeon did not intend to see her again.

She could not bear to look round at him again. Instead she let herself quickly out of his presence and almost ran off the unit. As she fled she knew that she was escaping from his defeatism. She could not allow herself to be contaminated by it. She had to believe in what she was going to do. She had to have strength for both of them.

Sue Craig had been frantically busy ever since Sister Brown had gone off for her three weeks' leave. And now Mr Schaffer had just been in to inform her that they had found a live donor for Dr Duncan and that he would be going to theatre tomorrow morning, first thing. The identity of the donor was to remain confidential Sue had been told, but that side of things would not concern her anyway. The donor would undergo a simple nephrectomy, or removal of the kidney, and would then be nursed post-operatively in the general surgical ward down the corridor.

Sue would be engrossed in caring for the recipient of the kidney, making sure that he was 'specialled' day and night until the crucial first two weeks were safely over and the new organ functioning properly. She would watch vigilantly for the slightest signs that his body was rejecting the new kidney, and monitor the output of urine and the introduction of an immuno-suppressive drug regime which would help to prevent rejection of the kidney, hopefully for the rest of his life.

The first post-operative danger would be infection, and the patient would be reverse-barrier nursed in his cubicle so as to prevent any avoidable contamination of his immediate environment by bacteria or viruses. The tight control that Sue would keep over his care would be relaxed only gradually as his hospital stay progressed and if things went well for him.

Trust all this to be going on while Claire was off, Sue thought, as the registrar, Tony Fraser, approached the nursing station. She did not have time for a long session now. It was almost supper time for the patients. Why was it that medical staff remained so totally oblivious to the normal routine of the patient's day, she wondered.

Sue had felt irritated with Dr Fraser for some time, and she did not know quite why. She admitted to herself that she had secretly hoped that Tony and Claire might be forming a romantic liaison and her hopes had been shattered by the obvious coolness that had existed between the pair after their return from the Lake District. Sue felt sorry for Claire and she frankly blamed Dr Fraser for any failure of their budding romance.

As Tony sat down on the edge of Sue's desk she could barely disguise her tongue click of annoyance at his presumption, but one glance at him told her that it was a worried man who now sought her attention.

'How are you off for staff tomorrow, Staff?' he inquired.

Sue found the off-duty list and handed it to Tony.

'Not too bad at all, as you can see,' she responded.

'Will you be able to special Dr Duncan yourself. Personally, I mean?' he asked.

'I was not planning on doing so. I have a senior staff nurse who I was going to allocate to his care . . .' Sue said.

'I'd really like it to be you. If that is at all possible,' Tony told her.

It was an extremely unusual occurrence for a member of the medical staff to insist upon a particular member of the nursing staff for a certain job, and Sue was somewhat taken aback by the surgeon's request.

'I shall try to be available,' she replied, 'but the other nurse is just as competent as I . . .' Sue was too professional to be easily flattered by the implication behind Dr Fraser's request.

'I have no doubt of that,' he said hastily, 'it's simply that I would rather that it was you.'

'Very well,' she said slowly. Dr Fraser got up tiredly from the desk and wandered off down the unit. He was relieved to have secured the best nurse for David Duncan's post-operative care.

'I'll be in to see him as soon as I get out of theatre,' he told her over his shoulder. 'Thank you, Sue.'

Sue could not put her finger on Tony's mood. Tomorrow's surgery was special, she knew that, but there was something else about it that made her experience something of the nervous feeling that she had sensed in Dr Fraser just now.

Much later on, as she made her way off duty, she put her head round the door of the doctors' room, half expecting to find it empty. But the renal surgeon was still there, sitting on the side of his own desk, some casenotes unread on his knee.

He looked up at her and Sue caught the full impact of his haggard exhaustion, behind his surprise at seeing her.

'Shouldn't you be getting an early night?' she asked, as brightly as she could. Then, almost as an afterthought, she said, 'I've been in with Dr Duncan, just giving him a pep talk before his op tomorrow, and I've promised him that I'll be there to welcome him back after theatre and look after him—at least for the first day.'

Dr Fraser smiled at the staff nurse.

'Thanks. That's great. See you tomorrow,' he said.

'Goodnight,' Sue rejoined, 'Sleep well.'

It was odd that he should be in such a strange mood this evening, she mused as she went out through the darkened corridors of St Helen's. She could imagine how much the operation on Dr Duncan was going to mean to his friend, but Dr Fraser should have the greatest confidence in Mr Schaffer's ability to perform a perfect operation. And all the registrar would be responsible for, after all, was a simple nephrectomy on some unknown donor.

Claire felt herself falling under the influence of the anaesthetic. The injection that she had been given in the ward had released her miraculously from all the worries that had been plaguing her for days and weeks; worries about the safety of her secret from the staff on the Renal Unit, about Fiona and Tony's concern for her and Sue's ability to cope with the unit. But, most of all, worries about the well being of David Duncan.

Now, with the anaesthetist's disembodied voice floating around her, Claire was sure at last that her decision was being acted upon and that, whatever happened from now on, she would have done what she most wanted to do.

Not even her natural apprehension over imminent surgery could dull the bright hope which she harboured within her that this operation and the one that she knew was beginning next door would mean new life for David Duncan.

Not even the memory of his cold, grey eyes and the terrible contempt for her which she had seen there stilled the excitement that Claire now experienced as her promise to him was about to be so secretly fulfilled.

Her last awareness as the anaesthetist's Halothane gas drowned reality, was of serenity and a peaceful fulfillment of purpose.

Next door, David Duncan too closed his eyes with calm composure, blocking out the masked face of the anaesthetist whom he vaguely recognised from operating lists of his own. He was resigned to whatever fate had in store for him, his resolve undermined and his determination vanquished by the long years he had suffered at the hands of his remorselessly slow, killing kidney disease.

He regretted little in life. But now his mind was filled with the vision of the face of the girl who had overseen his care during the last weeks; the girl whom he had met so long ago and whose care for him personally he had so remorselessly murdered.

One by one, incidents paraded themselves before his fading consciousness, each illustrating more vividly than the last the riches of which he had deprived himself. He knew how bitterness had blunted his reason and all his human feeling, and he hated himself for his own weakness.

If he came through this he would have to find a way of telling her how sorry he was, he thought. He . . . But the anaesthetic was working on his higher senses, blurring his thoughts and claiming him, sucking him down into deep unconsciousness.

In the adjoining operating theatre, Tony Fraser had begun to work with swift precision. He asked for instruments with quiet authority and did not utter a single non-essential word until, forty-five minutes later, the operation was completed and the kidney ready to be rushed next door. The operation had gone without a hitch and as soon as he was satisfied that Claire's condition was good, Tony changed, showered and joined the team next door.

He arrived at the chief's side just five minutes after the kidney that he had removed had been delivered for transplantation. Mr Schaffer was working with powerful concentration and the atmosphere in the theatre was electric. The operating team was large, but there was a blanket of tense silence over them so that the theatre felt almost empty.

An incision was made in the right lower quadrant of the abdomen. This would be the site for the new kidney. Mr Schaffer worked with deft deliberation, parting tissues with the greatest of care to produce a new hollow, a home for the kidney in the peritoneal cavity. The sooner the new organ could be connected to the patient's own blood supply the sooner normal function would be restored to it.

The left kidney had been taken from Claire as was Mr Schaffer's habitual preference when performing kidney transplants because the much longer vessels on this side facilitated surgery.

An hour later the hushed figures were still clustered around the draped form of David Duncan in Operating Theatre One, while Claire was just becoming aware that she was back in her bed in the surgical ward.

'How are you feeling, Miss Brown?' a staff nurse was asking her.

Claire opened her eyes and tried to focus on the unfamiliar face swimming above her.

'It's all over,' the nurse went on, 'you're back in your own bed and everything's fine.'

Claire tried to speak but could not because her throat was so dry.

'Don't try to speak now,' the staff nurse said, 'I'll get you an ice cube to suck until you can take a sip of water, later on. Are you feeling sick?'

Claire shook her head.

What seemed like an eternity passed before the nurse returned with an ice cube wrapped in a gauze swab. Claire felt its welcome freshness against her parched lips.

She had only one coherent thought in her mind and that transcended the discomfort of which she was aware in her side, her desperate thirst and her post-operative confusion. She wanted to know how the other operation had gone and whether David Duncan was all right.

Her mind worked over and over the idea while the staff nurse gently washed her and changed her out of her operating gown and into one of her own clean nightdresses. She saw that the staff nurse's fob-watch read two o'clock in the afternoon. His operation should be over by now.

After washing and settling Claire the staff nurse gave her an injection of Omnopon to keep the pain, which had begun to rise above the diminishing effects of the anaesthetic, at bay. To try to ask questions after this was impossible and Claire slipped into a semi-sleeping state.

Waking again, Claire was surprised to find that the sun had left her room. The ward outside was very quiet. She noticed that the drip which had contained blood when she had been returned to the ward was now running through with saline and she took this as a hopeful sign that it would soon be taken down altogether.

She was considering this possibility when a nurse quietly entered her room.

'Ah, you're awake. Would you like a little water? You

can have twenty mils—hardly a lake, but better than nothing!'

Claire smiled.

'Lovely. Thank you,' she said and gratefully accepted help to sit forward and sip her water.

'This can come down as soon as the saline's run through,' the staff nurse continued, indicating Claire's drip.

She busied herself with Claire's routine observations.

'And there's somebody here to see you when I've finished with you,' the nurse told Claire.

It was a joy to see Fiona's smiling face.

'How did you manage to get to see me today, so soon? Claire asked her flatmate.

'Special dispensation,' Fiona grinned, 'the sister on this ward was a good theatre nurse when she was a student!' Fiona winked. 'How are you feeling?'

'Amazingly good,' Claire told her truthfully. 'I hear everything went well.'

'So I hear.' Fiona put a bunch of daffodils down on Claire's locker.

'Thank you, Fiona,' Claire smiled.

'But what about . . . ?' she began to ask the irresistible question.

'I don't know about that,' Fiona told her friend, 'I haven't seen Tony or had a chance to speak to him today. Hasn't he been in to see you yet?'

'No,' Claire said, unable to keep the disappointment out of her voice.

'Try not to worry about it . . . I'm sure it went well for Dr Duncan. You've got to concentrate on getting strong yourself, Claire. Try to think about yourself for a change.'

Claire smiled at Fiona. If only she could understand how fundamental to her recovery was the knowledge that David was all right and on the mend too. It was agony not to know, to be unable to ask. She could think of nothing else and her imagination filled in only too vividly the gaps in her knowledge.

In the hours that she had lain under the influence of the Omnopon Claire had dreamed disturbingly of David and woken, shivering, unable to divide dreams from reality. If anything happened to him now she would not even be told, but worse, much much worse, she would feel in some way responsible. Perhaps surgery was to prove to be far more dire an alternative for David Duncan than his battle for life with the help of the kidney machine. Perhaps if she had not offered to be tissue-typed he would not ever have had to undergo such major surgery, and perhaps he would have preferred to live the way that he had been living.

'Sister did say only a minute and I don't want to abuse the privilege of seeing you this afternoon,' Fiona was saying, 'so I'll be off.'

'Thank you so much for coming,' Claire said.

'See you tomorrow. Is there anything you want me to bring in for you?'

'No. I think I've got everything I need,' Claire said, 'but some news . . .'

'I'll ring Tony tonight,' Fiona promised, 'now sleep well and don't worry.'

But Claire did not have to wait until the next day to find out how David's operation had gone. She did not know that Tony had already been in to see her earlier in the day while she had been asleep. He had not disturbed her but had checked her nursing notes and had spoken to the ward sister about her post-operative progress and told her that he was to be notified if there was any untoward change in Claire's condition.

Soon after the night staff had reported on duty, the nurse who was in charge came into Claire's room with someone behind her and Claire recognised the white-coated figure as that of the Renal Unit Registrar. Her heart jumped at the sight of him.

'Tony!' she exclaimed, 'Is everything all right?'

'Yes. Everything is going fine. Both operations went very well,' he pronounced significantly, 'and you're both doing well post-operatively.'

'Oh, good,' Claire managed to murmur, all the strength gone from her voice in her relief, 'I am so pleased.'

So, the first milestone at least was over. The long path ahead was not going to be straightforward for David, and the dangers of rejection would never be past for him, but at least the operation had been a success.

'He's not had to go on to the kidney machine?' Claire ventured.

'No,' Tony replied. 'The kidney you gave him worked straight away. And it's working still. Now it's just a matter of good nursing care and keeping our fingers crossed.'

For the first time since he had entered her room, Claire noticed how pale and tired the registrar looked. He seemed, with his stooped shoulders and haggard form, as if he were quite literally carrying the weight of the world.

'You must rest, Tony,' Claire said with sudden concern, 'you look exhausted. And thank you for being such a skilled surgeon.'

He smiled at her for the first time.

It was a most peculiar realisation for Claire that she had been operated upon by her old colleague a few hours previously, and it sounded odd to her own ears to hear herself thanking him.

'I've never had a more important patient,' the registrar told her thoughtfully, 'nor a braver one.'

Claire did not answer. She was choked with the irony of her situation. She could not help thinking of another doctor; the one from whom she longed for the recognition which Tony had just voiced. If only David Duncan thought her brave, or important, or even simply worthwhile . . .

She knew a pain greater than that inflicted by any surgical operation; the knowledge that David Duncan despised her and had valued her only fleetingly since his reappearance. Her face and mind still burned with the memory of his fierce passion, the interludes that had interrupted momentarily the cold uninterest with which he had treated her during their short reacquaintance.

Claire knew that she was powerless to change his attitude towards her and yet it seemed that the more distant he became from her the more she yearned for recognition from him. And the more she struggled to banish him from her affections the more certain she became of her overwhelming love for him.

How was she to live the rest of her life like this, knowing this one true chance of happiness had passed her by? Claire lay in her hospital bed in the empty room, and her thoughts echoed around inside her head. She would compromise, she thought, just as millions of others did. Tony Fraser had intimated that she was worthy of his romantic attentions after all, perhaps there would be others.

She remembered the Lake District; conversation, sunlit walks, pleasant meals together. And yet, something inside her rebelled against the idea of a romantic attachment to Tony, just as it had at the time. Anyway, now he was going out with Fiona. And as for the possibility of other men . . . Claire could not imagine where or who or why they might ever exist for her.

She drifted into uneasy sleep, only to be woken by a night nurse who came to take her blood pressure, pulse, and to check her drainage bottles. The nurse was anxious that Claire should take something to help her

sleep, but Claire refused all medication. She did not feel
that the small amount of pain she had justified Omnopon
again, and she did not want to take a sleeping tablet. She
had seen too many people go out of hospital addicted to
these supposedly harmless pills, and anyway, she
wanted her mind to be as clear as possible. If she was
going to have a sleepless night, at least she wanted to be
able to think through it.

Tony walked wearily back to his small room in the
residency, let himself in and sat down heavily on the
narrow bed. He rubbed his eyes with both hands and
then left them there, covering his face and blocking out
the world.

Around and around in his head rang the words of his
friend David Duncan; his first coherent words after he
came around from the anaesthetic:

'How is the donor?'

Tony had registered the question with cold shock. He
could not possibly know. There was no way in which he
could know who the donor was.

'Fine. Doing well,' he had answered at last, trying to
keep his voice normal, cool, professional.

'You operated?' David Duncan had asked.

'Yes,' Tony had replied.

'Where is the donor? Surgical side? Here?' David
Duncan had persisted.

'Yes,' Tony had responded, his panic mounting.

'Man or woman?'

'Hey, give it a rest, old man,' Tony had managed a
casual shrug and even a short laugh. 'What does it
matter, anyway? Main thing is that you're both all right.
You should know better than to strain yourself with all
this deep thinking straight after your op.'

Thus, Tony had managed to deflect his old friend from
asking any more searching questions. But if this was

what he had been like a few hours after coming off the operating table, how on earth, Tony wondered, was he going to cope with David for the rest of his post-operative hospitalisation. He was obviously not going to be prepared to let the welfare and identity of the donor of his new kidney remain a mystery to him.

Tony had not foreseeen this. He had underestimated David Duncan, even after all these years. He had forgotten what the man was really like, the caring, feeling man, beneath the anguish and anger of his chronic sickness.

All the time Tony had been with Claire this evening, he had wrestled with the problem of whether or not she should know that David had asked about her. And now he wondered for how long he could keep from David Duncan the truth about his operation. He knew that were his friend by some extraordinary chance to guess the truth, he would be unable to lie to him. There might come a moment, Tony realised now, when Fate might override medical ethics.

CHAPTER EIGHT

CLAIRE awoke on the Friday two weeks later and smiled sleepily at the night nurse who had brought her an early morning cup of tea. The sun was already shining palely into her room, illuminating splashes of colour, the get-well cards and the flowers. The side-ward had taken on some of Claire's personality and had become comfortingly homelike to her.

'Well, today's the day,' grinned the night nurse.

Claire sat up and blinked at the nurse. Then she remembered. How could she have forgotten? She was going home today!

'You hadn't forgotten? I don't believe it!' laughed the nurse.

'I slept so well last night, I honestly didn't remember until just now,' Claire rejoined. She sipped her tea with pleasure.

'You can have an early bath if you want to,' the nurse told her, 'before the day staff come on. As long as night sister doesn't hear you. She'll be in for her last visit in half an hour or so.'

'Promise. I'll be discretion itself!' Claire said. 'What's the time?'

'Six-thirty,' the nurse replied. 'Shall I run your bath for you?'

'Please,' Claire responded.

She felt so fit she could hardly credit that she had undergone fairly major surgery just two weeks before. The long scar in her left side had healed perfectly. She had lost some weight, but she did not mind that, and she felt as strong and healthy as she had done before her kidney had been removed. In fact, she felt fit enough to start work again right away, but instead she planned to take a week convalescing in Scotland at the home of her beloved spinster aunts.

She thought about Edinburgh while she lay in her bath; the lovely spired city where she had spent so many idyllic holidays as a child. She wondered how much it had changed, if at all, and how she would feel walking its streets again. She had avoided the place for years now, much to the distress of her aunts, because its streets were crowded with memories for her. She remembered having had the same forebodings about returning to the Lake District, but in the event her fears had proved unfounded. She dearly hoped that the same would be true of her impending visit to Edinburgh.

Back in her room, Claire chose a bright red dress from the three outfits that she had in the hospital with her. The red reflected her bright mood and would offset any pallor in her complexion, she decided. It felt like years since she had breathed fresh air and felt the cool wind on her face.

She stood in front of the mirror and brushed her hair until it shone with soft copper lights and then she piled it up on top of her head in a thick shiny knot.

By the time a nurse brought her breakfast, Claire was sitting in the sunshine in front of her window looking more like a member of the senior nursing staff in her office than a patient awaiting discharge from the ward.

Too excited to eat, Claire drank two cups of tea and waited for Fiona, or the ward round, or both. She could not leave until the doctors had seen her for a final time and she knew that Fiona was going to come and collect her, in spite of her insistence that she could find her way back to the flat perfectly safely on her own.

'Hi! Ready?' Fiona burst into the room after a very perfunctory knock.

'Ready,' Claire confirmed with a grin back at her friend.

'Doctors been round yet?' Fiona asked, sitting down on the chair she had pulled up next to Claire's.

'Not yet,' Claire answered, 'but I shouldn't think they'll be long.'

She suddenly experienced the reality of her going home and with the realisation the ward seemed so safe, so secure, so protected from the outside world.

'Is it cold outside?' Claire asked Fiona, trying to dispel her strange feelings with the question.

'Pretty chilly. It gets better when the sun gets higher, but it's still cold early on in the day,' Fiona replied.

Claire shivered involuntarily.

'You'll be warm enough in that, though. We'll take a taxi to the flat anyway,' Fiona said.

A murmur of voices outside the side-ward made both girls look up expectantly at the door and a soft tap on it heralded the doctors, accompanied by the ward sister. They clustered around Claire, smiling their appreciation of how well she looked. Sister complimented Claire on her dress.

'Ready for off, are we?' the consultant asked kindly.

Claire heard the old remark addressed to her as she had heard it asked of so many of her patients and the thought made her smile to herself.

'I think so, sir,' she responded politely.

'Dr Ahmed tells me that you've healed nicely and been doing all the right things. But how do you feel in yourself?' the Chief went on.

'Really very well, thank you,' Claire replied.

'And you're not going straight back to work? Lifting and so on?'

'No. A week's holiday first,' Claire affirmed.

'Well, you'll need to keep off the lifting once you do

get back to work. Or you'll do yourself real harm,' the senior doctor told her authoritatively.

Claire was about to promise that she would indeed take care of herself when she caught sight of Tony for the first time that morning. She was not particularly surprised to see him on the ward round as she was really his patient, but she was surprised by the look on his face. He looked really upset about something.

While she answered the chief, she could not help noticing that Tony was trying to catch Fiona's eye. While Claire spoke, Fiona and Tony slipped out of the room and disappeared out of Claire's field of vision. The chief's questions and kind admonishments seemed to go on forever and Claire could hardly concentrate upon them in her preoccupation with what was going on between Fiona and Tony Fraser.

Claire's mind began to run riot. Something must be wrong. It must be David Duncan. Something must have happened to him and Tony was telling Fiona not to let her know. Panic rose and flooded her. She could feel herself starting to tremble with the strain of continuing her conversation with the consultant surgeon. She felt that at any second she would lose control and push her way out of the small room to where she knew Fiona and Tony were huddled in the corridor talking in hushed voices . . .

'Well, good luck and goodbye for now,' the chief was saying.

'Goodbye, Sister Brown,' the ward sister was saying. 'This is the note for your general practitioner. And thank you for being such a good patient.'

Claire smiled distractedly at the throng of doctors with the sister in its midst, and watched impatiently as the group trickled out of her presence. She stood and followed them to the door of her room.

'Here you are, Miss Brown . . .'

A woman in a pink nylon overall was handing her a huge bouquet of flowers.

'Oh, they're not for me,' Claire stated flatly, looking past the woman for Fiona and Tony.

'But you are Miss Brown, are you not?' the woman asked, her voice and face both bearing the same kindly patience. 'It's on your door. Your name, I mean,' she explained.

'I am . . . I mean, yes, I know, but there must be some mistake,' Claire faltered absent-mindedly. 'You see, I'm going home today. This won't be my room much longer.'

'No, I know, I couldn't help overhearing the doctors and sister saying goodbye to you, dear. But these are for you all right. "Miss Claire Brown", it says on the note.'

Claire held out her arms numbly and the bouquet was placed gently in them, like a newly-born baby. She was completely at a loss to understand who would send her such an extravagant gift just as she was leaving hospital.

'Well, thank you, so much,' Claire said.

'You're welcome dear,' the kind woman from the WVS said, 'somebody knows how to say it with flowers, anyway! Lovely, aren't they?'

She waved cheerily as she disappeared towards the wards doors, leaving Claire staring down into a mass of cellophane-wrapped red roses.

Suddenly she became aware of two figures standing on the other side of the doorway. They were watching her quietly, with unreadable expressions on both their faces: Fiona and Tony.

Without speaking, Claire unpinned the little envelope that was attached to the cellophane of the bouquet and took out a tiny square of card from inside it.

'Thank you,' she read.

Her mind seemed to fall through space and then land gently upon an alien planet. So the impossible had happened; the unthinkable was true. David knew.

After a moment Claire looked up from the perfect blooms to the couple who stood nearby. Now she understood what they had been saying to one another. But how? How had it happened?

Tony read the question in her eyes.

He shrugged imperceptibly and then gave Claire a nervous smile.

'He guessed,' Tony said, his quiet words so simple, so shattering, 'he just guessed.'

'I'll go and see him,' Claire breathed, but she suddenly felt terribly faint.

'Not yet, Claire,' Tony's firm voice was accompanied by his arm encircling her waist, while Fiona took her flowers from her. 'Today, at least, you rest in the flat. This is enough for one day . . .'

Claire would never forget the taxi ride back to Monmouth Gardens that day; the bustle of the busy Friday morning townsfolk in the streets around them, the noise of traffic and children, the calm, reassuring presence of Fiona in the front of the car and the crimson glow of the roses, alive and vibrant beside her on the back seat.

She was surprised by how weak she felt after a few hours outside the confines of the hospital. She had been allowed to leave the ward towards the end of her second week, but she had only ventured to the hospital shop on one occasion fearing being seen and asked what she was doing in St Helen's during her leave.

Instead of going into the Kidney Unit to see David Duncan the day after she had been discharged, which had been her immediate plan, Claire accepted Fiona's plea to take things easy for her first day. They walked together in the park for an hour and the fresh air and exercise was quite enough for Claire to be glad to get back into the flat.

But having conserved her energy for one day, she felt

able to make the journey back to St Helen's hospital on the Sunday afternoon before she left for Scotland on the Monday. She reckoned that, with a bit of luck, Sue would take Sunday as one of her days off. She knew that she would never be able to hide the true reason for her visit from Sue, whereas the other staff would readily accept that she had simply popped in to collect some things from her in-tray in preparation for her return to work.

In fact, she need not have worried, for Miss Humphreys had chosen that Sunday afternoon to summon all the most senior staff from their areas of responsibility for an informal meeting to discuss the introduction of a new nursing strategy known as The Nursing Process. There had been a series of meetings chaired by the Nursing Officer on this subject over recent months, often with guest speakers. Claire had found it relatively natural to incorporate the new method of individualising care into the working of the Renal Unit but she was aware that ward staff were finding it more difficult to assimilate the new way of working.

The meeting meant that Claire was able to slip unnoticed into her sitting-room on the unit the following day. She picked up a pile of memos and papers from the tray on her desk and then straightened her back and stood, bracing herself for whatever the next few minutes would bring.

She had a sudden desire to abandon her plan; to skip the visit to David Duncan and simply walk or catch a bus straight back to the flat. Why should she lay herself open to more suffering on his account, even if it was only as a result of his indifference?

But an overwhelming powerful force drove her out of her sitting-room and towards the double doors that led into the unit and to Dr Duncan's bedside. She had admitted to herself the true nature of her feelings for this man, and those feelings fuelled her current action. Even if Fate decreed that their destinies were to be separate, Claire knew that she must see David Duncan once more, not just as his nurse but as a woman. The roses that shone on her dressing-table in the flat represented a gesture towards her to which she knew she would not be able to respond naturally once she was back in uniform.

But it was both as a nurse and a woman that Claire was shocked when she entered David Duncan's room. Tony had led her to believe that he was recovering uneventfully from a successful operation, and yet the only positive sign of health that Claire's expert eye could detect about the surgeon now was that he was not connected to the kidney machine.

The lean form in the bed before her was still, the fine dark head motionless upon the pillow and the face deathly pale. His eyes were closed, but something about the tension in his limbs told Claire that he was not asleep.

His eyelids flickered open and his face changed visibly as he recognised the person who had come into the room. She waited with dread for his response to her presence, her heart beating in her throat, choking her.

'Claire?' the surgeon asked uncertainly, as if he did not trust his own eyes.

'Yes. Lie still, David. I'll sit down here near you.' She drew a chair over.

Dr Duncan abandoned the attempt he had begun to lift himself up in the bed. He stared at her and the silence between them became unendurable to Claire.

'The flowers were beautiful,' she managed to tell him, the woeful inadequacy of her words plain to her even as she spoke them.

'I shall never be able to thank you properly,' he responded in a strange voice.

Claire met his look and her heart turned over. The troubled tenderness visible in his grey eyes melted her whole being.

'I don't want thanks,' she said, her voice strangled with emotion.

She was thinking that if this moment lasted and he did not avert his gaze from her, she would gather him to her, or fall into his arms, and the monstrousness of the idea, here, filled her with impotent anguish.

'But I want to thank you, Claire . . .' he whispered, 'I want . . .'

But his words were stopped by the intrusion of something else into his consciousness.

'Whatever is it?' Claire blurted out, unable to control her immediate alarm. She was relieved when in the next instant the professional in her took over.

David Duncan had closed his eyes as if to exclude her from his private pain. A frown gouged his forehead into deep furrows and, as Claire watched, beads of perspiration gathered in them.

She flew to the bottom of his bed where his nursing notes lay and had soon absorbed enough information from them to feed further her anxiety.

Dr Duncan had been feeling generally unwell since early that morning. He had been nauseated and dizzy according to the notes. There was no apparent inflammation, local swelling or tenderness over the site of the new kidney, but a spike on his temperature chart and a corresponding rise in pulse rate gave Claire an unmistakable and dreaded picture. This combination of signs and symptoms could mean infection or worse, much worse, rejection of the grafted kidney.

Claire moved back to the head of the bed. Curbing an instinctive desire to touch his forehead, she thought how ironical it was that, had she been in uniform, she would have done so without hesitation.

'It's just a slight headache,' he pronounced. But his face told Claire more.

'I'm going to leave you now,' she said, very gently, 'and I'm going to ask the nursing staff to give you something for your headache.'

'Claire, wait,' he said. He tried to place a restraining hand on Claire's arm, but his hand ended up holding her own instead. She felt his strong touch, as sure as it had been when he was well, but more sensitive than it had ever been during the tempestuous interludes of their recent relationship. In his touch she felt the David Duncan of five years before and the realisation made her feel faint.

'I want . . .' the surgeon began again.

Claire bent down so that her hair brushed his cheek. His voice was almost inaudible, 'I want you . . .'

The sentence remained unfinished. David Duncan's fingers released their grip on hers and she gently removed her hand.

Claire left the cubicle quickly, shutting the door softly behind her, and walked blindly to the nurses' station. Her mind was occupied with the single thought of getting care to David quickly and of getting him over this crisis.

The cluster of nurses at the station looked up, obviously surprised to see her on the unit.

'Will one of you go and attend to Dr Duncan? Now, please? And can somebody be allocated to special him for the rest of the day? I think Dr Fraser should be called up to see him too. He will want to take some blood for antibody tests and some urine for protein analysis. And I think his observations should be carried out quarter-hourly from now on . . .'

The urgency in Claire's voice had a galvanising effect on the two staff nurses present, one of whom immediately left for Dr Duncan's bedside. The other one looked up involuntarily at the clock above the nurses' station.

'Yes, I know it's only ten to four and you did readings at three o'clock,' Claire said, abruptly, 'but I'm worried about the patient.'

'Yes, Sister Brown. Of course,' the staff nurse said respectfully.

'Can I do anything else for you?'

Claire realised that this was a veiled allusion to her unofficial presence on the unit in mufti and during her leave.

'Oh, no thank you, Staff. I came in for some things and simply popped in to check up on Dr Duncan. I'm off now. See you a week tomorrow.'

Her flippant words and the friendly smile with which she delivered them belied Claire's true feelings. She was wondering how she was going to endure the next week, hundreds of miles away. There would be no way of knowing how things were with David Duncan. The thought lay inside Claire like a black hole, an awful void into which she knew she had to step.

Claire awoke with a start, glanced at her watch and realised that she had been asleep for an hour. The lady with the kind face sitting opposite her was still asleep, and the sun shone through the train windows into her silvery hair.

They must be very near the border with Scotland, Claire thought, and, as if the driver of the express had read her thoughts, the train slowed down enough for her to read 'Carstairs' on the station platform through which they were passing.

Carstairs meant only one thing to Claire; the grim, high-walled village hospital that held high-security psychiatric patients. She had often wondered, as a child, about this frightening place, but now, as a nurse, she was full of awe for the staff who dedicated their lives to caring for the inmates.

Ironically, the grim hospital marked the beginning of Claire's favourite part of the train journey to Edinburgh from the South. Only a few miles further North, the track found the sea and followed it for mile after lovely mile of undulating sand dunes.

She watched the sun fall into the reddening sea and drank a cup of coffee. Then, her heart calmed by the sight she had just witnessed, she read until the train drew into the huge iron central station at Edinburgh.

Waverley Station was full of memories for Claire. Mostly they were of her childhood terror of losing hold of her mother or father's hand and being lost in crowds of travellers and their tearful well-wishers and welcomers.

But, this evening, Claire experienced only pleasure at the sight of her two diminutive aunts awaiting like twin sparrows under the great glass-domed arrivals hall, and she greeted them with joy before walking, an aunt on each arm, up the broad ramp to Princes Street.

Before her in the evening light, the fine street unfolded in silver and green. The massive presence of the castle at the far end was grand and reassuring; the gracious sweep of the gardens which led to it elegant, and the spire of the Scott monument seemed to beckon Claire into the city. She felt a thrill of recognition and belonging.

'I hope you'll be comfortable, my dear,' said Aunt Sophie. It had apparently been her job to prepare Claire's room for her, while Sophie's sister, Sarah, had been allocated the task of preparing menus for each day of Claire's stay. Claire was touched by the excitement and enthusiasm which her visit had prompted. It offset some of her guilt at not having come before to visit her elderly relatives.

'I've left it much as you always had it, so I hope you're

not upset by the memories,' Sophie said, describing the bedroom she'd been given.

'Oh, no. I won't be,' Claire assured her. 'I have only happy memories of holidays with you both.'

And the old house, just as she remembered it, did fill Claire with happy memories and further reinforced her pleasure at being back in the 'Athens of the North'. The chintz-covered furniture and curtains, the little round mahogany coffee tables and the spacious garden were all the same as they had been in her childhood. Her room smelled of lavender, just as it had always done, and Claire was touched at the sight of a set of silver-backed hairbrush, comb and mirror which her aunts had placed on the dressing-table. They were those that had always been left out for her mother.

The next morning Claire awoke refreshed and feeling better than she had done since before her operation. She got up, bathed and went down to breakfast in a new sprigged cotton dress, feeling that spring had really arrived at last.

The aunts were seated at the small kitchen table which was laden with brown bread, butter, marmalade, tea and a jug of golden forsythia from the garden. A plate with an egg cup on it had been laid for her.

'You'll be having a proper breakfast while you're here,' Aunt Sarah stated, 'for I'm sure you'll not eat properly when you get back to England and start your work again.'

The aunts had a special way of making England sound as if it existed upon another planet from the one inhabited by themselves. The feeling it gave Claire was not purely one of pleasure; she had woken with a slight sense of unease which it had been difficult to banish and which the mention of England brought painfully back.

David could be much better by today—or he could be much, much worse. The only slight comfort that Claire had was the knowledge that she had at least seen him and been able to mobilise his care right from the beginning of his deterioration. This had been mere luck Claire knew, and the thought that her last minutes with him might have been snatched from her by a vengeful Fate chilled her to the bone.

She had known that she would not be able to tolerate this week if she allowed such thoughts to penetrate her consciousness, and she had struggled to banish them. But she had not succeeded.

The perfectly boiled egg that her Aunt Sarah served her, and the thin slice of bread and butter that she managed to eat with it, tasted like sawdust in her mouth. She bravely chatted, but her mind was elsewhere.

'And what are you going to do today, my dear?' asked Aunt Sophie brightly as she cleared the breakfast things away and began to wash up.

'I thought I'd take a walk and then do a bit of weeding for you. I love gardening and never have a chance to do any in Elchester,' Claire responded.

'Oh, that'll be fine,' her aunt murmured approvingly. 'We two are getting so old and stiff and I can't mind when we last tackled the weeds on the rockery, can you Sary?'

'That I can't,' said her sister placidly.

Claire smiled. She knew that Sarah hated gardening and avoided it at all costs. The result of Sophie's valiant single-handed gardening was a wonderful wild wonderland of shrubs, rhododendrons and cascading broom, relieved by a small patch of lawn and a magnificent rockery—her pride and joy.

Claire was soon within sight of the centre of town. She had walked up from the Georgian part of the city until, glancing over her shoulder, she could glimpse the silvery waters of the Firth of Forth in the distance. Much as she loved her aunts, it was nice to get out on her own and to be able to think her own thoughts uninterrupted.

She had to plan how her life would go from here. It seemed that she must break her bonds with Elchester, or certainly with St Helen's Hospital, for to stay there would mean that she would always run the risk of bumping into David Duncan. She could not bear to contemplate this possibility hanging over her future. If he recovered completely he would be sure to continue with his relatively new job at St Helen's, at least until he had completed his two years as a Senior Registrar. Only after that would he think of seeking a consultant's post elsewhere. The only way to protect herself from her unrequited love for David Duncan was to get right away and try, somehow, to start anew.

The smell of freshly-brewed coffee assailed her senses, and Claire looked down to see a basement coffee house, its door welcomingly open. Next door was a newsagent and Claire absently bought herself a newspaper. She often did this if she wanted to be left alone to reflect on her own thoughts. It was surprising how often lonely souls would come up and share her table and open their hearts to her if she sat unoccupied.

She got a cup of coffee from the counter and sat down with it at a table from which she could look up into the street and at the passers-by. It was a forgotten luxury to sit like this, in the middle of the morning, part of the real, non-hospital world of fit housewives and chubby babies.

She had turned to the middle of the *Scotsman* without taking in a single word. But now her mind suddenly flew to familiar words and she found that she was reading an advertisement for vacant nursing posts at a large hospital in the centre of Edinburgh. She registered the unusual fact of seeing nursing posts advertised in a daily newspaper. They must be quite adventurous in their outlook, she thought. It was mandatory for all posts in nursing in the National Health Service to be advertised in the two national nursing journals, but only an imaginative—and wealthy—health authority chose to broaden their search in this way. Claire was intrigued.

Three posts were vacant, all of them senior, but it was the third and last to be mentioned that held her attention. It invited applicants for the post of Second Sister in charge of a 'progressive' Renal Intensive Care Unit where 'pioneering transplant work' was being carried out in conjunction with the nearby University Faculty of Medicine.

It was true that Claire had held the only sister post on the Renal Unit at St Helen's and that this post might appear to be a demotion, but the fact was that St Helen's was a relatively small provincial hospital and that this post was in a much bigger and more important University Hospital.

Claire pushed her empty coffee cup away from her absent-mindedly. As she folded the *Scotsman* she decided to apply for the job. She went up into the sunny street and into the shop where she had bought her newspaper and purchased writing paper, an envelope and a pen. Then she went back down to the coffee house and took a second cup of coffee.

Half an hour later the application was safe in its sealed envelope. At the end of her letter she had explained that she was actually staying in Edinburgh for the next few days and that normally she resided in the South of England—though she very much doubted that she would be asked for an interview. The job was prestigious. There would be plenty of well-qualified applicants for it.

Her coffee finished, Claire went once more into the sunshine and walked down the hill until she came on to Princes Street itself. It looked lovely today. Her steps took her over the broad street and on to the garden side, and then up the Mound past the Scottish Academy of Art. She threaded her way up a steep winding close between the old houses beside the main road and emerged out of the dark shadows on to the Royal Mile. From there she walked the last fifteen minutes to the Royal Charitable Hospital, stopping twice to check her direction with passers-by.

Once inside the huge doors of the place she allowed herself a moment or two of awed amazement at the marbled splendour that surrounded her; the pale busts upon their plinths, the sweeping shallow staircases and the lofty ceilings, and then she found and followed signs to the Nursing Administration Office.

She posted her application directly into the box marked for incoming matter beside the polished oak door, and walked anonymously away, emerging five minutes later into the outside world again.

As soon as she was outside Claire felt as if she had acted in a dream. Only the certainty that that would be the first and last that she would ever see of the Royal Charitable Hospital kept her from running back and retrieving her letter somehow.

While she wandered, window shopping through the town, Claire became more and more horrified at the mental aberration that had led her to behave so uncharacteristically. She was not normally prone to such drastic, spontaneous moves as the one she had just made.

To think of applying for a job here when even the rest of the week spread out before her never-endingly! It was only Tuesday. There were another six days before she would know how David Duncan was, and by then . . . by then, anything could have happened.

Banishing the worst from her mind, Claire knew that it would be at least three months before the hospital would release the surgeon from its care, and that then there would have to be weekly follow-up attendances for the next nine months.

She had to be there until he was discharged. The desire to get back to his bedside was almost too much for her. Claire went over again and again the words he had last spoken to her and she felt she would die herself if anything had happened to him during her absence.

She had managed to compose herself by the time she got back to her aunts' house. An afternoon in the garden would be perfect, she reflected as she walked up the front path to the door. She would be able to forget everything except the earth she worked upon.

'Claire? Is that you, dearie?' Aunt Sarah called the moment she had opened the door.

'Yes, Aunt, I'm just back,' Claire returned.

'There you are. Well. I've got some salad on the table for you . . .'

Oh, dear, Claire thought, how am I going to cope with all this love and attention?

'Thank you,' she said, smiling at her aunt, 'That'll be lovely.'

Then her Aunt Sophie appeared, agitated and chattering like the sparrow she so closely resembled.

'Tell her then,' she fluttered at her sister. She had obviously been listening to her conversation with her niece.

'It'll wait until she's had her food,' said Sarah impatiently.

'It'll not,' Sophie exclaimed. 'The Royal Charitable Hospital's been on the telephone for you, Claire. I can't think what they want. But there's a name, Miss Ferguson or something. I can't mind exactly. And she'll be expecting you to call back this afternoon.'

All this was delivered in a breathless gush. Claire was stunned with the efficiency that this represented, but also with the *fait accompli* with which it presented her. She would have to return the call to the Nursing Administration Office.

The whole of the lunch was taken up with trying to calm the aunts. Claire had discovered that she simply could not keep the truth from them, and had had to admit to her madness of this morning. They were over the moon with the idea that their niece might actually move up to Scotland to work at the famous hospital in their city, and Claire had difficulty in convincing them that the likelihood of her getting the job was minimal.

'We'd like you to come for an interview, Miss Brown,' said the soft voice on the other end of the line that afternoon, 'while you're here. It'll save a great deal of trouble on all our parts. Now, when would suit you? Friday morning would be fine with us.'

'Oh, yes,' Claire heard herself agree, 'that would be fine. When shall I come?'

'Now, let me see. I think half past nine would be fine,' the lilting voice returned, 'so we'll see you then?'

'Thank you. Yes,' responded Claire, 'and thank you for telephoning me, Miss Ferguson.'

'Not at all. Goodbye for now,' the Senior Nursing Officer responsible for personnel replied.

Claire put the telephone down, a sense of foreboding competing with the thrill of excitement that was spreading through her.

It was not until she got into bed that night and tried to sleep that the full impact of what had happened hit her. All night long she watched the stars through her bedroom window. Those same stars were hanging in the sky above St Helen's Hospital in Elchester. If only she could know how he was. Perhaps he was lying awake now, just as she was.

But she could not imagine his thoughts. She longed to feel his skin again and to look into his eyes, even if they were the cold, clear eyes of indifference. Nothing mattered except being near to him. If only she were not too late, she could endure any displeasure on his part just so long as she could help him over the next weeks and months, until she knew that he was safe.

The train drew out of Waverley Station with a purr and Claire waved as her Aunt Sophie wiped a tear from the corner of her eye with a lace-edged handkerchief on the receding platform. Aunt Sarah did not cry, but waved energetically back at her niece with a look that said 'don't worry, I'll look after her for you'. Claire smiled. She had been well cared for during her stay. She felt well and strong and thankful to her aunts for all they had done for her.

But, as her aunts disappeared from sight and the train gathered speed, Claire allowed herself a private sigh of relief. At last she was on her way back to Elchester. She would be back at work tomorrow, Monday, and she could hardly wait to see St Helen's again—or more accurately Dr David Duncan. Her heart rose to her mouth at the thought of him.

She did not expect to hear again from the Royal Charitable Hospital. They had been very kind, and she had been impressed by the interview. But she had interviewed very badly.

For a start she had been negative about when she would be prepared to take up any new post, insisting that she needed longer than the statutory month to hand in her notice at St Helen's. She had explained the staffing situation on her Renal Unit and the truthful fact that the nursing staff tried to give much more than one month's notice of their impending departure from the Unit.

Miss Humphreys would not object to her leaving quickly and Claire knew that she would respect the desire of any member of staff to leave to go to another post, but the fact was that Claire would not feel comfortable leaving suddenly. The reasons she gave the interview panel were all honest and truthful enough. But she had omitted her personal reason for wanting to stay in Elchester until the summer.

And then she had fairly limited professional experience. The Renal Unit at St Helen's was her first sister's post and she had been at pains to point this out to the SNO, Divisional Nursing Officer and Senior Sister who had interviewed her.

But, in spite of all her negativity, she had detected more than just polite interest on the part of the nurses at the interview. They had asked her a good deal about her attitude towards counselling both patients and other members of nursing staff in the highly emotionally-charged environment of a unit which cared for the young chronically sick.

Claire's answers had resulted in nods and smiles and note-taking. Claire's deep commitment to this aspect of nursing could not but have been apparent to the panel of interviewers.

'What do you consider the most significant contribution to the preparation of the patient undergoing renal transplant surgery as far as nursing staff are concerned?' the Unit Nursing Officer had asked Claire.

Her mind flew back to her response and she realised with what conviction she had delivered it!

'Oh, the psychological preparation,' she had declared, 'as much time as is needed must be spent with each patient, tailoring encouragement, education and emotional support to his individual needs and requirements . . .'

And now, speeding southwards, Claire thought bitterly about how she had failed in this very task with at least one of her patients. She had been unable to get near to Dr David Duncan, let alone help him to come to terms with his surgery and the future he faced as a result of it. Claire could only hope and trust that Sue had managed where she had failed to get him to talk about himself.

She could not know how the surgeon had built his desire to live directly upon the sacrifice she had made for him. She could not imagine the hours during which Dr Duncan had cross-questioned Tony Fraser over Claire's operation and post-operative recovery.

She had no way of knowing for how long Sue had sat beside the surgeon's bed while he, his eyes burning, had asked her when Sister Brown would return to the Unit, and how Sue had fought to calm his delirious ramblings and to soothe the agonised self-reproach which she sensed beneath them and could not understand.

CHAPTER NINE

SUE watched Claire slip through the double doors that led into the Unit. The sister had lost some weight and her new slimmer figure suited her. Sue noticed how glossy Claire's thick hair was and how poised and calm she appeared as she approached the nurses' station in her fresh, white dress. As she came up to Sue, a smile accentuated the pretty curve of Claire's mouth.

Sue had no notion of the turmoil beneath Claire's calm exterior; the inner agitation that Claire had suffered ever since she had awoken from her fitful sleep at six o'clock that morning. Her unease had been only momentarily allayed by the glimpse that she had caught just now of David Duncan as she passed his cubicle.

Obviously the rejection crisis which she had witnessed beginning before she left for Scotland had been arrested, but his changed appearance and confinement to complete bedrest chilled and alarmed Claire. He was obviously not out of danger yet.

She listened carefully for the thirty minutes that it took Sue to give her a full report on six of the seven patients currently on the Unit and her nerves were stretched to breaking point by the time Sue, with a sigh, reached for the bulging folder of notes that documented David Duncan's care.

'Dr Duncan is recovering slowly from the rejection crisis that he suffered six days ago . . .' Sue began. She looked up briefly and met Claire's dark brown eyes before returning to the notes in front of her on the desk.

'He had local irradiation of the graft on Tuesday . . .'

Claire's mind fled backwards to the Edinburgh coffee

house where she had sat that day, applying for a post in Scotland. What had she been thinking about? She must have been mad to even think that she could move away from Elchester in the foreseeable future. Sue's voice called her back to the present.

'The crisis was treated with immuno-suppressives and intravenous steroid therapy: methyl-prednisolone which has now been reduced to an oral dose of 200 mgs per day and will be further reduced to a maintenance dose of 20 mgs per day by the end of next week—if all goes well.

'His weight has remained steady for the past four days; his blood pressure is also stable and satisfactory, both lying and standing. Proteinuria is controlled and urine output volume good. His temp. is down now, but he was delirious and rigoring for twenty-four hours. I specialled him.'

Sue handed Claire a series of dated charts so that she could map Dr Duncan's progress for herself. Claire took in the grossly abnormal chemistry and haematology reports of a week ago, and the more normal recent ones. So, she thought, in spite of our compatibility in tissue type, he has had to go through all this.

'He's not out of the woods yet, but he seems to be over the worst now and all we can do is watch him like a hawk and hope that he doesn't try to reject again . . .' She was saying in conclusion.

Claire's mind, if not her emotional state, was ordered when she entered Dr Duncan's room a few minutes later. She knew that her face did not betray her inner feelings when she greeted the surgeon in soft, professional tones. But he did not return her courtesy.

'How are you?' she persisted, but David Duncan again ignored her.

His discomfort in her presence was apparent to Claire. She understood, at least in part, why this should be. The massive doses of steroid drugs had produced the characteristic flush across the features whose pallor had been so imprinted upon Claire's memory. Dr Duncan had the cruelly artificial appearance of vigorous good health that the anti-inflammatory drugs produced and he must be only too uncomfortably aware of his drastically changed appearance.

'When did you get back?' he charged her at last. He did not return the smile Claire gave him.

'This morning. An hour ago,' Claire responded simply.

'It's no good,' he said. Claire swooped on the remark, recognising the opening to his feelings that he had never offered her before.

'You're going to get well,' she told him. 'You're going to walk out of here in a few weeks' time a fit man.' The last time she had said similar words to him came back to her. The words echoed around her head after she had uttered them, as if she needed them to strenghten herself too.

The surgeon's doubt was written in his face.

'Don't do it, Claire,' he said. His words were spoken between clenched teeth.

'What?' Claire asked. She knew what he meant, but she wanted him to go on talking to her, even though his words cut into her like steel knives.

'Don't try to live my life for me. You've done all that you could possibly do for me. Now leave me alone. Please.' He spoke the last word with brutal finality and knew that she had no option but to withdraw from his presence.

But as she reached the door, desperation lent Claire the courage to speak again.

'I'm going to help you, Dr Duncan, whether you like it or not. That is my job here and I'm going to do it for you just as I would for any other patient.'

His stare froze her. Outside the door to his room,

Claire stood motionless for a moment, composing herself. She knew that no matter what the cost had been in trembling hands and inner confusion, she had told David Duncan the truth. She was going to accept the challenge of nursing him. She was not going to avoid his care.

Nothing existed for Claire outside the Unit over the weeks that followed. Fiona had tried and failed to get her flatmate to go out with herself and Tony some evenings and even once for a picnic over a weekend. But Claire seemed obsessed with work. She came off the Unit exhausted and went to bed early, awoke refreshed and headed back for St Helen's as if nothing else but the Kidney Unit mattered to her.

Both Tony and Fiona privately worried that she was working too hard, but far from looking the worse for all her efforts, Claire appeared to thrive on the arduous schedule she set herself. She gave up several days off and still seemed able to carry on energetically. In spite of not bothering to eat properly she looked fit and even more attractive than she had done before her operation.

Fiona, Tony and Sue were not the only people to notice Claire's behaviour.

'I don't think I've ever seen anybody work as hard as you do, Sister Brown,' David Duncan told Claire one morning as she finished charting his observations.

The surgeon had adopted a cool, off-hand manner with Claire which successfully distanced them from one another. He had not made even a remotely personal remark to her since that day that had marked the beginning of his deterioration, before she went to Scotland, and he always addressed her by her professional title. Claire had stopped feeling upset about his coolness towards her and had admitted to herself that, if anything, it helped her to care for him.

But there was no denying the softening in the surgeon's grey eyes this morning.

'I enjoy my work,' Claire told him frankly, momentarily thrown by the look in his eyes. It had been four long weeks since she had returned to work and she had concentrated all her mind and emotional attention upon effecting an improvement in the surgeon's condition. Now at last she was content that this was underway.

'That's evident,' the surgeon told her now.

'And it's rewarding when people get better,' Claire said, replacing his charts at the end of his bed. It was slightly unnerving to be having an informal exchange of words with him. He was sitting in an armchair beside his bed, apparently relaxed, his good looks more and more evident to Claire as his illness receded.

The surgeon closed the book he had been reading and placed it on the bed beside him before he spoke again.

'Especially when they've been such thankless so-and-sos to nurse,' he stated in a quiet voice.

Claire took a deep breath.

'Oh, one doesn't need thanks to encourage one,' she managed to say in a level voice, 'not at all.'

'Nevertheless, it must be nice to get some,' the surgeon went on.

Claire felt the blood rising to her cheeks and a lump in her throat.

'But people do appreciate you,' he stated. Claire realised how soft his voice had become.

'Yes,' she murmured, 'I know that they do.'

She was glad when the moment was interrupted by the loud tones of her bleep, summoning her to the telephone at the nurses' station, but she had to tear her eyes away from the grey ones which held her spellbound in David Duncan's presence.

Hours later, in her bedroom in the empty flat, Claire went over and over the few minutes of that day that

really mattered to her. Every word Dr Duncan had said
had stayed fresh in her memory, in spite of two emergency admissions, a bad-tempered interlude with Tony
Fraser over documentation and an even more bad-
tempered ward round with Miss Humphreys, all of
which had contributed to one of the most frantic days she
had had since her return to work.

The ward round stopped outside Dr Duncan's room.
Inside Claire could see the tall, strong figure of the
surgeon, standing with hands on hips, his back to the
door, looking out of the small window. It was a fine May
morning, eleven weeks after his operation.

Mr Schaffer, Tony Fraser, two housemen and two
medical students had packed themselves into the tiny
room. They were followed by the slight figure of the Unit
Sister who was forced to watch proceedings from the
open doorway. But her distance had compensations: she
could observe, unobserved, and as the surgeon turned to
face his medical colleagues, Claire absorbed the full
impact of his physical recovery.

He looked younger, fresher and more handsome than
he had looked since she had first known him. His thick,
dark hair shone with health and his face was relaxed,
humorous. As she looked, the surgeon gestured towards
the narrow bed, neatly made, and the single armchair
that comprised all the furniture of the cubicle.

'Do sit down,' he invited his colleagues with a broad
grin.

Claire dragged her gaze away from the handsome
features and found Dr Duncan's notes in the trolley
which she had had to leave just outside the cubicle. She
handed the bulky folder to Mr Schaffer.

'So you're getting pretty sick of our inadequate hospi-
tality, eh?' the Chief quipped in return as he glanced
through recent additions to the notes.

'Oh, I wouldn't say that exactly . . .' Dr Duncan's eyes twinkled as he replied and Claire realised with a shock that he was looking directly at her. She looked quickly away in her confusion.

'Well, you can maybe take another week of it?' Mr Schaffer asked the surgeon lightly, 'And after that I think we can let you go.'

Claire's heart missed a beat and then resumed its painful rhythm in her chest. She had expected this news, after all. Why did it come as such a shock to her?

'Marvellous!' Dr Duncan smiled. Claire caught the nod and wink that passed between the surgeon and Tony Fraser. It said all there was to be said about the friends' relief and pleasure. It also epitomised the feeling which Claire knew she should herself be experiencing in place of the numb loss which filled her.

'But you'll need to be followed up of course, every week for nine months subsequent to discharge from here. I assume you know about this?' Mr Schaffer inquired.

'Yes, sir,' Dr Duncan responded. 'Is there any reason why follow-up visits should not be made to another unit in another part of the country? Always assuming that the staff there liaise properly with those here and that you approve, of course?'

The Chief Renal Surgeon absent-mindedly scratched his head while he considered this request.

'Er, no. I don't think there would be any problem in that. In theory, anyway. We'll need to discuss at greater length where you are proposing to go and for how long; what local facilities are available and so on. But we can do this later, when there's more time,' the Chief told his patient.

David Duncan nodded his approval.

So he was leaving Elchester. The significance of the recent exchange between the surgeon and Mr Schaffer came home to Claire with awful clarity. The rest of the ward round and the remainder of the morning passed in a blur. She had been so sure that she had prepared herself adequately for the departure from the Renal Unit of Dr Duncan; she had known all along that he would only need three months hospitalisation if all went well for him. And she had done her utmost to ensure that all did go well for him; to achieve precisely this outcome. Yet the imminence of his departure filled her with dread.

It was half past four and Claire was on her way off duty when the surgeon signalled to her from his room.

'Claire,' he spoke her name as she entered his room.

'What can I do for you?' she asked. She hoped that her formal response successfully masked the thrill that his calling her by name had produced in her.

He was sitting on the edge of his bed, his long legs stretched out in front of him. He was casually dressed in a grey checked shirt and cord trousers which accentuated his athletic build. His outdoor attire accentuated for Claire how naturally the outside world would claim him and how inevitable was her loss now that he was ready to leave the Unit.

'I want to tell you something that I have discovered about nurses over the past weeks. It is something that I never knew before,' the surgeon began.

'Oh? What is that?' Claire asked politely. At least he found her worth talking shop to. The rare bitter little thought flashed through her mind, surprising Claire with its violence.

'It is,' he continued, 'that some nurses nurse with only a part of themselves. The patient quickly becomes aware of that,' he paused and sought her eyes with his own so that she was forced to return his look, 'while others nurse with all of themselves. This latter sort are those whose very presence is therapeutic; the touch of whose hand is healing. They are very remarkable, gifted people . . .'

Claire let the lilting voice break over her. She felt she could drown in the new liquidity of his sea-grey eyes and yet a part of her was tugging her away, trying to make her run, escape from the reality of him and retreat into the privacy of her own tormented thoughts.

'You are one of those gifted people, Claire.'

She fought to find her voice. 'I did not think I was able to help you very greatly,' she slowly said at last.

'No,' the surgeon corrected her quietly, 'it was I who was unable to help you. It is not easy to accept things from someone to whom one can offer nothing in return.'

Claire struggled to understand and he shook his head before he went on patiently.

'I want you to understand how sorry I am for my past behaviour.'

'You do not have to apologise to me, Dr Duncan,' Claire stumbled over the words. 'I must go now. I am on my way off duty . . .' Claire made blindly for the door.

She managed to hold back her tears until she had made the comparative privacy of the main corridor out of the hospital, but she could not stop them from streaming down her face as she walked home through the early summer sunlight. They were a bitter-sweet admission to herself that she longed for more than simple professional appreciation from David Duncan.

The first thing that Claire did when she made up the off-duty rota for the following week was to ensure that her own days off fell over the day that Dr Duncan was due to be discharged from the unit. She could at least spare herself the agony of watching him leave. It was easy to arrange; there were plenty of staff at the moment and she had not requested special off-duty for herself for ages—ever since her leave three months ago.

Claire forced herself to get Dr Duncan's remarks of the other day into perspective. She knew that it was only natural for patients, even the most difficult patients, to begin to openly express their gratitude as their condition improved. It was normal too, for them to become emotionally more open and responsive to their nurses the nearer grew their release from the hospital. Claire had forced herself to acknowledge the fact that she had witnessed such behaviour in countless patients, and that Dr Duncan was surely no exception.

She had persuaded herself too not to read too much into his flattering words; not to see anything but simple relief and genuine gratitude in those grey eyes. And yet, as the end of the week drew near, she found it increasingly difficult to go into his room. The moment arrived, though, when she had to do so.

'I shall not be here tomorrow when you go,' Claire told Dr Duncan as she was about to leave the Unit for her days off, 'Staff Nurse Craig has your prescriptions and referral notes ready for you, as well as a letter for your general practitioner. She'll be here in the morning. Good luck, Dr Duncan. I hope all goes well for you from now on.'

The words she had prepared so carefully sounded stilted and hollow. They seemed to emerge unnaturally as if uttered by a wooden doll.

'You are off-duty tomorrow?' David Duncan asked, apparently ignoring everything else that she had said.

'Yes,' Claire returned.

'Fine,' the surgeon replied matter-of-factly. 'Goodbye,' he said.

Claire walked home, unaware of anything but that final, dreadful word. She heard Fiona come in late that night. The hushed voices of her flatmate and Tony Fraser seemed to go on and on, and Claire was glad when she realised that it had got too late for Fiona to make her customary goodnight call at her door.

Eventually, as the birds began to welcome the new day, Claire fell into a restless sleep. A few hours later she viewed her ravaged face in the bathroom mirror with despair. Her eyes were red and swollen-lidded, her cheeks blotchy. She felt ugly, tired and drained.

She ran a bath, got into it and began to try to get her thoughts into order. With an effort, she decided that all that had happened was what she had expected to happen and been prepared for. All she now had to do was to learn to live with the reality of David Duncan's absence from her life. If that was going to take time she might as well begin the process straight away.

Her hair washed and feeling fresher, Claire dressed in clean jeans and an old comfortable T-shirt. She could not manage to eat anything but she made herself a pot of tea and sat at the kitchen table drinking it. It was still only nine in the morning. Fiona must have left unheard for her early duty at seven.

Claire found the park full of birdsong. Ducks and swans jostled one another on the still surface of the pond and pairs of doves cooed in the trees. Beds of glowing pansies and the pink torches of the chestnut trees drew her attention away from her inner thoughts.

She sat on a park bench for some time. There was a great deal worth living for. She was young, fit and had a career. She could build on these things. Leaving the park and the noisy shopping streets of Elchester Claire found herself heading for the bus station. There she boarded a bus, full of women with bulging shopping bags. She chose it because it had 'Willowedge' written up at the front and she liked the sound of the name.

Three quarters of an hour later, Claire alighted on the edge of a picture book village green. She began to explore her surroundings, losing herself in her delighted discovery of an old forge with a working blacksmith, thatched cottages and a post office that looked as if it came straight out of *Alice Through the Looking Glass*.

She was amazed when she discovered that it was already four o'clock in the afternoon and that the next regular bus back to Elchester left in half an hour's time.

She took a final stroll around the village green.

On the bus Claire decided that she would take another magical mystery tour the next day. If only she could concentrate on a book for the rest of the evening she thought, if Fiona was out again, then the first day would be over, she would have proved that she could cope, and it might be easier from now on.

Nevertheless, she was really disappointed to find the flat empty when she got back. She supposed that Fiona must have met Tony straight after work. Claire knew that the Renal Unit was not particularly busy at the moment, and these light evenings Fiona and Tony had been going out earlier. She found herself envying them and at the same time wishing there was somebody at home to talk to.

She wandered aimlessly from room to room and then forced herself to stop her restlessness and to sit down with a book. She opened the sitting-room window allowing a cool breeze to blow in, carrying the scent of newly-mown grass from the park. As she breathed in the smell, the sound of the municipal mowing machines stopped and the world seemed suddenly very quiet and she had the disquieting sensation of being all alone in it.

The doorbell made her jump. A glance at her watch told her that it was just after seven. Fiona must have forgotten her keys. Claire was so pleased at the thought of seeing her flatmate that she almost ran down the stairs. The front door swung open and Claire looked up breathlessly into the clear grey eyes of Dr David Duncan.

'Aren't you going to ask me in?' he asked, smiling
calmly at her astonishment.

'Of course.'

He followed her up the stairs and into the flat in
silence.

The sitting-room looked suddenly pretty, with shafts
of evening sunlight falling in through the open window
and lighting pools of colour in the carpet.

'It's nice to see you in a neutral setting again,' Dr
Duncan said quietly, 'in spite of your impressive professional performance.'

The compliment was obviously genuine, and Claire
allowed herself a brief nervous smile. She felt terribly
vulnerable, and was completely at a loss to understand
why the surgeon had come to her flat.

'Can I get you something to drink?' she asked.

'Er, no, thanks. I've brought my own.' He opened the
carrier bag that he had brought with him and took out of
it a dark green bottle of Moët et Chandon champagne,
'but I think we could probably do with an ice bucket and
a couple of glasses. Oh, and these are for you, too.' He
handed Claire a posy of freesias.

Claire stared at the bottle then at the flowers and at
last allowed herself to meet the amused look of her
visitor.

'What is all this?' she asked at last, with quiet control.

'It is to say thank you, Claire, and more . . .' David
Duncan stood opposite her, just a couple of feet away,
the champagne still in his right hand, his eyes burning
into hers. 'It's to say please help me to forget the past
and live the future. I want to make a fresh start, Claire,
and I want you to make it with me . . .'

Claire felt her knees threaten to give way and she sat
down slowly on the settee before they did so. She could
hardly believe that her own powerful imagination had
not conjured this scene out of the fresh summer air, but

the smell of newly-mown grass and freesias bound her to the reality of her situation.

'I want to leave Elchester, Claire,' he was saying. 'And I want you to come with me, if it is not too much to ask of you.'

Claire listened silently, still hardly trusting her eyes and ears.

'I had nothing to give you until now, Claire, nothing to offer you but life with an invalid. All these years I have watched you and as my feelings for you grew, so too did bitterness at the illness which threatened my life and made me a virtual cripple. You have changed all that, Claire. You have given me life and hope. Please share it with me.'

He put the champagne down gently, next to where Claire had lain the flowers on the table, and drew her to her feet. He held her tenderly, close to his body. She felt as if she would melt into him.

'I need you so much,' he whispered, 'a lifetime will not be long enough in which to love you.'

The sweet smell of Claire's hair assailed his senses and he could hardly hold back the tide of his long-contained passion.

Claire succumbed to the tightening of David's embrace. Nothing existed in the world except for his arms, the smell of his skin and the laundered shirt through which she could feel his heart pulsing next to hers.

She was totally unable to resist the response her body made to his and, for the first time in her life, she was not afraid of it. She shivered as his caressing hands found her shoulders, her neck, her breasts.

When at last he kissed her, Claire tasted the exquisite taste of his love for her. She had dreamed of this kiss, yearned for it and despaired of it ever being hers. Now that it was, she wanted it never to end. At last they broke away from one another, until it was she who sought his mouth again.

After a few moments she drew away from him, half-ashamed, half-afraid of rejection or contempt. She searched for them in his eyes, but she found there only care and the clouding of his passion.

David stood back from her and took both her hands in his. They stood looking at one another as if they were seeing one another for the first time.

'David?' Claire whispered at last.

'What?' he asked, 'what's wrong Claire?'

She smiled at the concern in his face and because, at this moment, there was nothing in her world but joy.

'I'm thirsty,' she told him.

David kissed her forehead.

He went into the kitchen and Claire heard ice clinking into glass. When he returned he was carrying an improvised ice bucket: a mixing-bowl full of ice cubes and two tumblers.

'All I could find,' he explained.

Claire grinned. David opened the champagne and it sparkled out, splashing into the tumblers, mirroring Claire's inner feelings. David handed her a glass and waited to drink a toast.

'Well?' he said.

Claire, glimpsing in him for an instant the shy young houseman whom she had once known, had to control an urge to put her glass down and kiss him again.

'Yes,' she said instead. 'Yes, please.'

They sealed their promise with a kiss that tasted of champagne.

Much later, Claire remembered to ask David the question that had suddenly seemed unimportant earlier in the evening.

'Where do you think you want to work after we leave

Elchester?' she inquired. It was a blissfully lazy question. She didn't really care where they went and it was hard to believe that, just a few hours ago, the thought of his leaving St Helen's had been almost physical agony to her.

'I want to try for a Senior Registrar's job at the hospital where I trained,' David said, stroking her cheek thoughtfully as he replied.

'In Scotland?' Claire asked. She realised that she did not even know whether or not he had completed his medical training in his home country.

'Yes,' he said, 'in Edinburgh.'

Claire did not know why she should be surprised except that for some reason she had never entertained the idea that David might be from the one city in Scotland with which she was familiar. He saw her surprise.

'Do you know the place?' he asked.

'Yes. I went there to convalesce,' Claire told him.

It was David's turn to be surprised.

'Where did you get your clinical experience?' Claire asked. But in some strange way she knew the answer already.

'The Royal Charitable Hospital,' David said, 'Do you know it?'

'Well, not exactly . . .' Claire smiled.

David was smiling at her quizzically, waiting for her to go on. But Claire could not be bothered to explain everything now. She simply looked into his face and enjoyed the delicious prospect of sharing her life with him.

And, besides, they only had another five or ten minutes before they would have to leave the flat to join Fiona and Tony for dinner at the restaurant where a special corner table had been booked, and champagne ordered for nine o'clock.

Doctor Nurse Romances

The romantic gift for Christmas

First time in paperback, four superb romances by favourite authors, in an attractive special gift pack. A superb present to give. And to receive.

United Kingdom £3.80
Publication 14th October 1983

Darkness of the Heart
Charlotte Lamb

Virtuous Lady
Madeleine Ker

Trust in Summer Madness
Carole Mortimer

Man-Hater
Penny Jordan

Look for this gift pack where you buy Mills & Boon romances

Mills & Boon.
The rose of romance.